John Macgowan

The Life of Joseph, the Son of Israel

In Eight Books

John Macgowan

The Life of Joseph, the Son of Israel
In Eight Books

ISBN/EAN: 9783744712590

Printed in Europe, USA, Canada, Australia, Japan

Cover: Foto ©Raphael Reischuk / pixelio.de

More available books at **www.hansebooks.com**

LIFE

OF

JOSEPH,

THE

SON OF ISRAEL.

IN EIGHT BOOKS.

Chiefly defigned to allure young Minds
to a Love of the Sacred Scriptures.

BY JOHN MACGOWAN.

PORTSMOUTH, N. H.

PRINTED BY CHARLES PEIRCE.

1797.

TO THE PUBLIC.

THE *following History of the Life of* Joseph *was forwarded to me by a* Friend *in* London. *On perusing it, and finding the English Edition out of print, a number of persons have expressed an earnest wish of seeing an* American *impression of it. In my opinion, it is well calculated to instruct and entertain the rising generation, and as such will, I trust, be deemed an useful Book in our public Schools. The* BIBLE *is an inexhaustible Treasury of Divine Truth : whatever, therefore, is conducive towards promoting a* Love *for that* Blessed Volume *in the youthful mind, will undoubtedly meet with the Patronage of the seriously disposed of every* Christian Denomination——*The Author was a much esteemed Minister of the Gos-*

pel

pel in London, and, had he lived, *would
have profecuted his* pious *plan.** *Well
acquainted with his excellent character, I
could not, after being repeatedly requefted,
any longer deny the prefent editor thefe few
lines, expreffive of my warmeft approbation
of this valuable work ; fenfible that it only wants to be known in the United States
in order to be admired.*

WILLIAM ROGERS, D. D.
*Profeffor of Englifh and Oratory in the
College and Academy of Philadelphia.*

PHILADELPHIA,
Jan. 1, 1791.

* See the clofe of the Preface.

P R E · F A C E.

WHEN a new book is uſhered into the world, if it has the happineſs either to pleaſe or diſpleaſe, there is great enquiry made after the author :—— And as I think it would be a pity to forbid the world this pleaſing itch of enquiry, I forbear putting my name to the Life of Joſeph till ſuch time as this curioſity hath in ſome meaſure ſpent itſelf. Yet not to leave the reader altogether in the dark about who and what the author is, I ſhall give him a negative or two.

1. He is not then a writer who cannot err, for he thinks it poſſible for him now and then to be guilty of miſtakes, in ſentiment as well as literature. Conſequently,

2. He is none of that claſs whoſe *ipſe dixit* is the pure ſtandard of orthodoxy. But he has one thing to ſay for himſelf, which will weigh a great deal with peo-

ple

ple of fenſe and candour, and that is, that the Life of Joſeph is wrote as well as he could do it, for could he have done it better, he had never ſent it into the world as it is : for it was not wreſted from him by force ; neither got out of his hands by clandeſtine means ; by thoſe who were eager to ſee it in print, before he had time to put the finiſhing hand to it, as has been the unhappineſs of ſome other authors. He can aſſure the reader, that had his ability bore any tolerable proportion to his time and opportunity, the preſent production had been without a blemiſh.

But why did I chooſe any part of ſacred hiſtory for my theme, will be next aſked ? Did you not know that the Bible has been laid in a great meaſure aſide for many years paſt ? and that people of faſhion will contemn it, if it was for nothing elſe but being akin to ſcripture ? Yes, I know it very well ; but becauſe I have not ſeen a better book ſubſtituted in its room, I would gladly have the uſe of the Bible revived again. If writers were all agreed to keep to Bi
ble

ble fubjects, of courfe the readers muft ; for they can only ramble, as they are led by their author. The facred volume is fertile of fubjects, calculated both to pleafe and inftruct ; when let down, by proper elucidation, within the reach of young capacities. And rather than one clafs of readers fhould want entertainment, let me tell them, that the Bible contains many hiftories of love affairs. Perhaps this may tend more to recommend it to attention, than all befides, which I could fay.

I have fometimes thought, that, if inftead of ufelefs controverfies, upon points which the infinitely wife God never intended to be clearly underftood in this life, gentlemen of facred character were to employ their leifure hours in rendering fome part of divine hiftory pleafing, and eafy to be underftood by young ones, their lives would be fpent to much greater advantage than they frequently are. Much time and pains have been taken ; much zeal, as hot as Smithfield fire, has difcovered itfelf in defending that which never was revealed ; and in
explaining

explaining that which is inexplicable ; and many a flaming curſe has been thundered againſt thoſe heretics, who would not believe but upon evidence given. Whether my, writing the Life of Joſeph is not a leſs abuſe, both of the world and of my own precious time, I leave to the reader to determine.

Well, but what induced you to ſet about writing this ſame Life of Joſeph ? I tell you honeſtly then, that I was not prayed and intreated to do it, by people who thought me maſter of the ſubject, as has been the caſe with more reſpect-able writers : for no one perſon ever hint-ed ſuch an opinion of me.—But I wrote it merely to pleaſe myſelf, as the firſt party concerned ; and had fully gained my end, had I been as well pleaſed with my own performance as I was with the ſubject.

And pray what induced you to pub-liſh it, ſeeing the world is already bur-dened with more books than ever will be read ? In this alſo I differ very widely from many of my brother authors, ſome of whom ſeem to be objects of our warm-

eſt

eft pity. I have grieved, or might have
grieved, at the heavy complaints of fome
authors whofe labours have been taken
from them as it were by force of arms.
Such was the importunity of friends,
who had feen the manufcript, to have it
publifhed ; that they could not poffibly
refufe to gratify them, however reluctant
they were to appear in print in fo difcerning an age. But, alas ! I cannot
pay this compliment to the Life of Jofeph ; for to tell the truth, no one creature ever defired me to fend it abroad,
or fo much as to read one page of it in
manufcript.   The whole affair was fettled betwixt my honeft, and fince then
very unhappy bookfeller.*   Certainly
thofe friends act in a very unfriendly
manner, who oblige a modeft author,
contrary to his ftrongeft refolutions, to
print a performance which he has fuch a
very mean opinion of himfelf, and to expofe his reputation in genius and literature to the hazard of being bandied a-
bout, throughout the whole nation by
                                    thofe

---

* Mr. Jofeph Johnfon, lately burned to the ground in
Pater-nofter-Row, and uninfured.

thofe too mercilefs fets of waggifh re-
viewers ; who make nothing at all of
laughing at human folly.   Were my
friends wicked enough to expofe me to
fuch difagreeable hardfhips, 1 fhould
certainly renounce their friendfhip forever.   I might indeed fay that the Life
of Jofeph is *publifhed by requeft*, if I
thought it would promote the fale of it ;
but then I fhould mean the requeft of
my bookfeller, who had fome hope of
making a few pounds by it, if publifhed.
But Jofeph fhall go without difguife,
whether it fucceed or not.

What is the moft wonderful of all in
me is, I am not afraid to appear in print,
even in this age, difcerning as it is ; not
that I think myfelf cenfure proof ; very
far from it.   But I have a reafon more
formidable, ahd which effectually fe-
cures me from apprehending any evil at
the hand of the critic ; and that other
authors may attain the fame happinefs, I
fhall reveal the important fecret to them.
And it is this.   I fhall be glad to have
every fault in the performance pointed
out, that I may make the fecond impreffion

preffion more perfect than the firft; therefore the more curious they are in noting its defects, and candid in communicating them to me, the more fhall I deem the critics my friends.

Having given an account of myfelf, fufficient to fatisfy any reafonable reader, I proceed to obferve that I have a clafs of people in my eye, and for whofe fakes chiefly this little performance is fent abroad, amongft whom I hope to have even fome admirers. I mean the young and rifing generation, whofe felicity I hope I can fay I have very much at heart. If I can but get their good opinion, I care not who elfe fnarl at the Life of Jofeph. I have been much converfant with the geniuffes and tempers of young ones, both in my own family of feven children, and in a much larger fphere of action; and have had frequent occafion to mark with regret, that the harfh and fevere methods which many take with a view to form the young mind to agreeable habits, have quite the contrary tendency. I have an utter averfion to the crabbed countenance of

the

the cynical pedagogue, who has no other way of imparting inftruction but upon the end of his cane, or face of his ferula. If the terrible man, and terrible he is to the little lovely creatures, who fhrink as it were into nothing, and fhudder at his tremendous menace, would only confider that it is impoffible to divide hatred from fervile fear ; he would perhaps fee it neceffary to aim at gaining the affection of his young pupils, in order to infure his own fuccefs. Or if he himfelf would go to fchool to common fenfe, and learn to drefs virtue in its native attractions, and learning in its own innate lovelinefs, he might fpare the labour of the cane and ferula, enjoy the love & efteem of his pupils, inftead of their dread and hatred ; and return them to their parents good proficients in ufeful learning, inftead of branding them with the infamous name of dunce. A name however, that always proclaims the mafter's incapacity to teach ; and but very feldom want of ability in the boy to learn. Want of ability to learn is very rarely the cafe ; and want of inclination would

be

be much feldomer found than it is, if care was taken to entertain the fancy whilft we would inform the underftand- ing. If learning was made to refemble play rather than flavery, it would be- come a pleafure inftead of a burden.—— I never yet found that I could fucceed by mere precept and penalty ; but if I was happy enough to hit upon the turn of my pupil's fancy, I never failed of the defired fuccefs. Fancy is an active principle and will be employed, though in different fubjects it operates varioufly.

The Life of Jofeph is defigned to entertain my young reader, without vitiating his mind ; by fetting before him one of the moft amiable of facred characters, in the perfon of Jofeph, the hero of the ftory. I am not aware of having at all departed from the fpirit of the text, nor from the rules of proba- bility. I have indeed ventured upon a few conjectures & fictitious poffibilities, which fome very grave reader may per- haps be offended with ; but in this I am kept in countenance by the moft ortho- dox of our commentators, who all have

their

their fuppofitions and conjectures on many places of facred fcripture. It may
be, my young reader could even wifh
that I had more enlarged upon the fan-
ciful part of the ftory. To him I
would make this apology for myfelf.——
I wrote with caution, always keeping in
my eye the people above referred to, and
was cautious of offending them ; for I
know that it is poffible for a man to be
deemed an heretic, for a few things which
to them appear to be new and out of
the beaten tract of orthodoxy ; therefore
I had a reftraint upon my own inclination, which otherwife would have led
me to give a free fcope to my fancy.

Should The Life of Jofeph, the fon of
Ifrael, be acceptable to thofe for whom
it is defigned, I am not certain that I
fhall not fend fomething more of the
fame kind abroad into the world.

THE

LIFE

OF

JOSEPH.

ARGUMENT.

Jacob entertains his family with the history of his own life and that of his fathers—Joseph's private reflections upon it,—His first dream—His brethren's envy on account of it—Judah and Simeon's different reflections upon Joseph's dream—Reuben endeavours to remove their jealousy—Belphegor's resolution to blow the flame—Simeon's dream inspired by that devil—Joseph's second dream—His brethren's resolution to murder him—The patriarch's care about his sons—Joseph sent to enquire after their welfare—A Canaanite finds him and invites him to his tent, where he tarries till morning, and dreams an alarming dream—He departs for Dothan—His brethren consult about putting him to death—Reuben interposeth, is exposed to danger from their resentment, and is upbraided with defiling his father's bed—Joseph intercedes for his life in vain—Recites his last alarming dream in order to move their pity—Reuben dissembles with a view to divert his brethren's purpose and persuades them to cast him into a pit—Joseph's prayer in the pit: Abel the protomartyr appears to him, comforts and instructs him.

B O O K I.

IT was at the end of autumn, when the bounties of Providence were fafely gathered in, that venerable Jacob entertained his convened family with the hiftory of his own life, and the lives of his father Ifaac, and Abraham his grandfather. A ftory fo full of interefting incidents, related in a manner truly pathetic, fometimes excited the friendly tear, and at others the cheerful fmile, upon the countenances of his audience.—— None was more affected than pious Jofeph, who feemed earneftly to catch every fyllable in the narration ; little Benjamin indeed marking the emotions of his brethren's hearts, by their countenances, gave undoubted tokens of filial piety, as well as his elders. Jofeph, love Rachel's eldeft born, was abforbed

contem-plating

contemplating the viciffitudes experienced by his revered parent, and could not forbear fympathifing with him in every part of the hiftory, whilft tears bright as orient pearls ran down his cheek. Even when alone he could not but ruminate on the wifdom and goodnefs of the God of heaven, in fetting virtuous Jacob before Efau the prophane ; notwithftanding nature and Ifaac's choice feemed to have defigned otherwife.——Says he to himfelf, when alone, " Raw and unexperienced as I am, young and untaught either in the myfteries of religion, or the mazes of deceit among men of this world, I can fee a very wide difference between my father and my uncle Efau. A greater difference there was not between the roughnefs of the latter, and the delicacy of the former, when examined by experienced Ifaac's careful touch, than there is between their two minds, formed fo very different from one another. And who made, or could make the difference but God, from whom the fpirit of life originally came, and who formed them both in the fame maternal

nal womb. I adore thee, O my God, that the promise is with my father Jacob." Often did he reflect with pleasure and delight on the gracious visits, which the patriarch received from the Almighty at Bethel and Peniel. " Oh, said he, that this same God, the God of my father, may be with me even as he hath been with him ! that this God may be my God in the land of the living, and my guide and portion for ever and ever."

Thus meditating on the changes. through which providence had brought his father, and earnestly imploring grace to imitate the patriarchal conduct, he was seized by the lulling charms of balmy rest, and sunk beneath the superiority of the angel of drowsiness. As he slept he dreamed, and lo ! all his brethren and he were together in the neighbouring field, laboriously reaping the nodding harvest ; when to his amazement, the sheaf which he had last reaped stood upright in the midst, as a governor; and all his brethrens sheaves, as so many loyal subjects, hastened to pay their court,

court, falling down proſtrate before it.
Unacquainted with malice and envy,
and not knowing but his brethren were
as free from it as himſelf, he very innocently told them his dream ; but alas !
the diſtinguiſhed regard at all times
ſhewed him by his indulgent parent, had
already called up the demons of malice
and envy to poſſeſs their unequal hearts.
They heard him with attention, and felt
the impreſſion in their hearts, but could
not hinder the diſagreeable ſenſation
from diſcovering itſelf on their countenances ; ſo ſure an index is the countenance to the heart.   He, as a youth who
loves inſtruction, aſked them what could
be the meaning of ſuch a dream ? But
they diſguiſed their apprehenſions, and
with affected diſdain turned from him,
telling him they underſtood nothing of
the matter.   But no ſooner was he departed from them, than they entered into a conſultation among themſelves re-
lating to the affair.   Judah firſt began,
" My brethren, ſaid he, the dream which
the youth has related to us, however innocent and thoughtleſs he may be reſ-
pecting

pecting the event, appears to me ſomething more then the influence of mere
imagination ; and if my judgment is
not miſlead, it is ominous of ſuperior
dignity in the perſon of Joſeph, or the
dominion of his ſeed over the children
of his father." "For my own part, returned Simeon, I conſider the whole as
the fruit of ambition ; you know he has
been foſtered up in a vain conceit of
himſelf, by the overweening fondneſs of
an indulgent and doting parent. Seeing himſelf placed firſt in the paternal
affection, who knows but his pretended
dream is a ſcheme concerted to root himſelf the deeper in his father's heart, with
a view to ſupplant us of the patriarchal
bleſſing, as our father did our uncle E-
ſau ? Or, if he really did dream what
he has now related, is it not pretty plain
from thence, that it is owing to his
mind running upon the wiſhed for dominion ?" Reuben now rejoined his
brother Simeon thus, "the patriarch's
partiality towards Joſeph can never be
juſtified, for if brethren are expected to
dwell in unity, there muſt be an equali-
ty

ty among them; partiality in a parent
being the feed of certain diffentions a-
mong his children.   Yet we ought to
do the boy juftice, he is truly lovely in
his perfon; even in his opening graces
you may fee all the beauty of his mother, mingled with the mafculine gravi-
ty of our renowned father; befides, his
temper is amiable and mild, his manners
fweet and attractive; let us not then
load the good man with reproach, even
if he fhould love our brother with fuperior regard.   Our father was put before
his elder brother, and thereby the promife defcends to us, let us not, then, too
haftily condemn the youth, before we
know what the Almighty will do with
him."

THUS reafoned the fons of Jacob,
whilft Belphegor an angel of the damned race, implacable in his hatred againft
mankind in general, and efpecially a-
gainft the children of the promife, returning from a deteftable incurfion in
the neighbourhood of Jerufalem, drew
near and hovered in the air over their
heads, to acquaint himfelf with their
circumftances

circumftances, the better to imbiter their lot, if not precipitate them into ruin. .He was a witnefs to the perturbation of Simeon's heart, and refolved that the flame already kindled fhould not die, whilft it was in his power to throw oil upon it. What the malignant fpirit aimed at, was to excite him to embrue his hands in Jofeph's youthful blood, as before he had done in that of the Shechemites; which, as he concluded, if executed, would anfwer infernal purpofes in divers refpects ; that it would bring down the holy patriarch with forrow to the grave ; it would bring an everlafting reproach upon the chofen race ; and, it might provoke a juft God to vifit them with fome terrible judgment. To accomplifh this with the greater facility, he refolved to impofe upon his fenfes by a dream ; for which purpofe he watched him in his tent, and perceiving him in a deep fleep, he firft breathed upon his eyes an hellifh damp, that diffufed darknefs and horror thro' his whole foul. Then, directing his views to futurity, he difcovered Jofeph

in a chair of ftate, himfelf and his brethren proftate before him, intreating
mercy at his hand ; by and by he finds
himfelf bound in fetters, in the prefence
of his brethren, and caft into a dungeon ;
now he fees his own feed the drudging
menials of the feed of Jofeph. The
name of Jofeph is extolled to the heavens, and thofe of his brethren mentioned but with coolnefs, and fome of them
particularly his own, with abhorrence.
Withal he faw the behaviour of Jofeph's
children to be haughty and tyrannical
to their enflaved brethren. So did the
parent of error miflead his judgment,
by the delufion of an hell infpired dream.
Simeon awoke in the morning, and addreft himfelf to his paftoral care, following the fleecy race as they cropped
the verdent herbage ; but a fullen penfivenefs was fettled on his countenance,
the caufe of which he chofe not as yet
to reveal.

In the mean while Jofeph grew in
ftature, in the affection of his father, and
fear of his God. And ere long he
dreamed again, a dream of the fame im-
port.

port with the former.   He fancied himfelf, in a pleafant meadow, covered with the frefheft verdure, befpargled with the many coloured ftains of natural dye ; the lion, the leopard, and panther, were hid in filence, in their lonefome retreats ;—their nocturnal prowlings in the defart were fufpended, and only the voice of the nightingale was heard.   As he walked along, admiring the beauties of nature and adoring the fupreme Creator, he perceived an uncommon motion among the celeftial fpheres ; the fun, the moon and the feven ftars, flew fwiftly from their orbits, and came and made obeifance to him. The next day after evening oblations were offered up, and Jacob's family convened to fupper, fuch as the fimplicity of thofe days admitted of : unfufpecting Jofeph told his dream before them all. His father heard with thoughtful attention, yet deemed it prudent to conceal for the prefent his thoughts, not knowing what envy it might excite among his **brethren** ; and therefore gave him a flight rebuke, by faying, "Shall I and

C   thy

thy mother and thy brethren indeed come to bow down ourfelves to thee, to the earth?" The dream and interpretation of it had both taken poffeffion of the patriarch's mind, and, notwithftanding his reproof to Jofeph, he pondered it in his heart, and confidered it as divinely infpired, portending fome important event.

It was quite otherwife with Jofeph's brethren : this laft brought the former dream afrefh into their minds, and they began to fancy themfelves as almoft in fervitude to their brother already. The repetition of the dream encreafed their envy, and alarmed their apprehenfions : efpecially when Simeon, who had concealed his dream until now, had related it to them. They confidered the whole as fixed by fate, and faw but one way to prevent the execution of the decree; and that was (horrid to name) to cut fhort his period of life ; as if there had not been blood enough already upon their guilty fouls. Strange indeed that the parents of the chofen feed, fhould be found contending with their God,

and

and ſtriving to prevent the execution of
his purpoſes ! · How unſearcheable are
the ways of the Moſt High ! and his
judgments paſt finding out !

THEY now departed to their rural
employments, firſt to Shechem, where
the herbage was ſoon devoured, and
from thence to Dothan, where there was
plenty of graſs, and ſhelter for their cattle.   Unfurniſhed with that dutiful regard, due to ſo good a father, their departure was concealed from him ; whether from thoughtleſſneſs, or with a
view to find occaſion to deſtroy Joſeph,
I pretend not to ſay : but their abſence
filled the patriarch's mind with ſolicitous
concern for their welfare, wherefore,
he reſolved to ſend his beloved Joſeph
in queſt of them, to learn their ſituation.
In the mean while, being arrived in
Dothan, they conſult together what methods to take to prevent the grandeur
of their deteſted brother, and his death
was determined on by the majority.
Thus ſin at firſt diſcovered itſelf to be
exceeding ſinful by the horrid act of
fratricide, and now the iſſue of this coun-

ſel

fel was, that brethren fhould fhed their brother's blood, and without fo much as the allegation of guilt againft him.

JOSEPH was difpatched by his father to enquire after the health of his brethren, a tafk which was extremely agreeable to a mind like his, formed to offices of benevolence. Firft he went to Shechem, where he expected to have found them, but inftead of them he met with a ftranger, who, feeing a comely young man wandering in the fields, drew near and thus accofted him :— " Young man, if I miftake not you are a ftranger in thefe parts, wandering in queft of fome defired object; I am a native of this country, and if you will be pleafed to command me, I am ready to ferve you to the utmoft of my power. It is the will of heaven that we fhould not be neglectful of ftrangers, but perform all offices of good-will towards them, and we find our account in obeying the precept, for the God of heaven is the Guardian of ftrangers." Jofeph, affected with the goodwill of this ftranger, meekly replied : " My

friend

friend, for such your sentiments bespeak you, I am here at this time in search of my brethren, who should be feeding their flocks near to this place, I shall take it kind if you can inform me whereabouts they are." "If, replied the stranger, you mean the ten sons of Israel, the Hebrew, I can help you in this matter, for it is but three days since I was with them upon bufinefs; when finding the adjacent paftures confumed by their numerous flocks, I heard them conclude upon going to Dothan, where the earth produceth herbage in the richeft luxuriance."

"If you are brother to thefe godlike fhepherds, let me prevail with you to refresh yourfelf in my tent, which is at no great diftance; and in the morning as foon as the cheerful fun illumines our horizon, you shall depart in peace." The day being far advanced, and the fable evening drawing near, our youthful hero accepted of the kind invitation and flept in the tent of the Canaanite. Retiring to reft, his dreams came into his mind, earneftly he wifhed for the

C 2   interpretation.

interpretation of them ; but amidſt his
contemplations he fell aſleep, & dreamed one of a very different nature. He
fancied himſelf wandering in an unknown field, amidſt the nocturnal
gloom ; ſun, moon and ſtars, having hid
their radiance in the denſity of the at-
moſphere,   Penſive and melancholy, he
wandered with painful ſteps, he knew
not whither.   No voice was heard but
that of beaſts of prey, upon their night-
ly ravages, the growling of the lion, and
hooting of the bird of darkneſs were the
only muſick that ſaluted his ear.   Ere
he was aware, he fell into an horrible pit,
inhabited by hiſſing ſnakes, and other
deadly reptiles ; and in the fall, his many coloured coat was torn piece-meal,
and hung upon the buſhes over him.—
He had but juſt reached the bottom
when two monſtrous adders warped
themſelves about his legs, which fright-
ed him ſo that he awoke and rejoiced
that it was but a dream.   Some benevolent ſpirit of the ethereal race, having
heard the malevolent conſultations of
his brethren, might take this method of
apprizing

apprizing him of some danger near at hand, that he might guard himself a-gainſt their bloody deſigns. But Joſeph's friendly heart was incapable of ſuſpicion. He would have deemed it a crime in him never to be forgiven, to have entertained, but for a moment, the leaſt jealouſy of their humanity. Had integrity & uprightneſs equally govern-ed the reſt of thy ſons, O Jacob! What ſcenes of ſorrow wouldſt thou have eſ-caped, and how gently would time have conducted thee through the decline of life.

The reverſe of Joſeph's diſpoſition was theirs, for the moment they ſaw him afar off, they renewed their determina-tion againſt him to deſtoy him, and by one bold ſtroke to free themſelves from the fear of his future advancement.—— " According to our wiſh, cried raptured Levi, he comes ; behold this dreamer cometh !" returned Simeon, " Now is the time brethren, let us put him to death, and ſee what will become of his dreams." " Not ſo, replied Reuben, How ſhall we who have the adoption
and

and covenant, we who are the feed of
the promife, be guilty of fratricide ?—
What ! fhall we who are called to lift
up holy hands, and to offer pure oblations to the God of heaven, ftain our
fouls with the blood of an innocent
brother ? remember brethren, the blood
of Abel, cried from the earth to the
Lord to whom vengeance belongs, and
will not the blood of Jofeph roufe the
wrath of the Omnipotent ? And who
fhall efcape when an avenging God
purfueth ? Is our father partial in favour of the youth, the fault is not with
him. Even envy itfelf muft confefs
his merit. Are his dreams ominous of
his future greatnefs ? Cannot Jofeph be
great without our being flaves to him ? :
Shall we flay our brother for the licen-
tious rovings of unbridled imagination ?
Who can anfwer for dreams ? Could
we even convict him of ambition, might
not his youth and inexperience, in fome
meafure plead his excufe ? Further experience, growing acquaintance with
men and things, would teach him that
man is not originally defigned for flave-
                                                ry.

ry.   Let the old man our father plead
for his Joseph.   His life is wrapt up in
that of his child.   And will you dare to
murder the father in the son, and pierce
his heart thro' the blood of his Joseph ?
Think of our father my brethren ; see
him weeping a detested life away over his
murdered son ; murdered by the begot-
ten of his father ; murdered by the very
men in whom he confided without re-
ferve.   Let the fear of God, and the love
due to fo venerable a father, be advocates
for his helpless youth ; and let me never
fee the evil that shall by this villainous
barbarity be brought upon Ifrael, the
favorite of heaven."

"Is this Reuben,with malicious irony,
cried Levi, Reuben the firft-born of Jacob ?   The pious Reuben, who in a
phrenzy of brutal luft crept into his father's bed, and defiled it ?   Where was
thy fear of God, thy love and veneration for thy father then ?   Art thou our
dictator ?   Thou who couldft not fpare
even thy father's wife, all of a fudden
become fo pious ?   Art thou fo careful
for thy father's life, thou who alone
                                    hadft

hadft audacity to cuckold him ? Let
fhame for ever fhut Reuben's mouth,
and leave it to good men to be advocates for virtue."

" Your invective, my brother, faid
Reuben, ftings me with the keeneft remorfe. I own the charge to be juft and
cannot forget the evil of my fin. I have
difhonored my God, my father, and myfelf ; and have left thereby, an indelible
ftain on my offspring, to the lateft generation. But the heavy days and the many fleeplefs nights, that this foul mifcar-
riage has coft me, though they can never
extenuate my highly aggravated guilt
from before the God of Jacob ; might
in fome meafure exempt me from the
upbraidings of my brethren. Believe
me, Levi, my own confcience ferves as a
thoufand reprovers, and needs not your
cruel affiftance. Yet it is juft, my brother, and I cannot refent it. But my former impiety, is indeed the reafon wherefore I cannot fall into your bloody meafures. My confcience, too, loudly tells
me that I have guilt enough upon my
foul already, without contracting more
                              in

in fuch an horrid manner as this, which Simeon has prefcribed; that I have already been the caufe of more than enough of forrow, to my dear and honored father, without joining in the murder of his fon, to bring down his venerable hoary head, with infupportable forrow to the grave. He whofe confcience groans under the weight of inceftuous adultery, has little need to add to the burden, the tremendous weight of innocent blood. I cannot therefore confent to the deed."

"The indelible ftain which Reuben, by his own confeffion, hath fixed on himfelf and offspring, may reconcile the bafenefs of his mind to flavery, faid Simeon; but our feed is free, and not born to fervitude. Therefore, Jofeph, by my advice fhall die; if pious and reformed Reuben, will not confent to his death, he dies along with him. Why fhould he live to be able to accufe us to our father? One condition, and only one, if you are all agreed, I would have offered to Reuben; if he agrees to that he lives, and if not, he and Jofeph die together; for he fhall never be the publifher of our guilt.

Let

Let Reuben become our accomplice, otherwise bind himself by an oath to the moft inviolable fecrecy. By this alone can he hope to prolong his life. Speak, Reuben, do ye accept the conditions?"

" Give me till to-morrow about this time to confider of it, and then you fhall have my anfwer, replied Jacob's elder born."

"" One hour and no more we grant, at which time we expect your anfwer," rejoined the brethren in wickednefs.

By this time Jofeph came nigh to his brethren, and fmiling with delight at having found them all together, came near to embrace them, and inquire after their health. But what inexpreffible furprife feized him, when inftead of returning his careffes, they turned away from him, and fhook him off, with vengeance louring on their countenances? Inftantly he is feized, ftript of his rich party coloured coat, and fettered both hands & feet. Alarmed Reuben, cried, " Stop, ftay your hand but one hour, the hour promifed & ye fhall then have

my

my anſwer." All agreed that one hour
and no more ſhould be granted, ere Joſeph was put to death ; and Reuben
caſting a look of deſpair and pity on his
fettered brother ; " I wiſh, ſaid he, your
duty to your father, and love to your
brethren, could have admitted your ſtay-
ing at home, inſtead of viſiting theſe
men who are bent on your deſtruction ;"
ſo ſaying, he precipitately withdrew to
conſider what anſwer he ſhould deliver
to his brethren.

The elder brother gone, and Joſeph
encloſed amidſt his ſanguinary brethren,
like an helpleſs lamb amongſt ſo many
voracious wolves, was thus addreſſed by
one of them. " Ambitious youth !
think now of your ſtate, one hour elapſ-
ed and the tide of your ambition is for
ever ſtemmed, one hour puts a period to
your life, which is forfeited to our liberty.
Die you muſt and ſhall, if fate had de-
creed the contrary." He replied, " Had
I known the malignity of your inten-
tions, I might have avoided the ſnare ;
but duty to my father, and to my brethren, and therefore duty to my God brings

D　　　　　　　　me

me here ; if he hath led me hither for
flaughter, I ought, I muft fubmit, but if
my God fees it for the honour of his majefty to preferve me, he hath power to
change your purpofes, as he turneth the
rivers of water ; or may point out means
whereby I may be delivered from your
vengeance.   Tell me what I have done :
wherein I have offended you :   If I have
erred, it is unwittingly, and it is hard to
be put to death for inadvertency.   Make
known my faults, and if I reform them
not, let loofe your fury upon me.   But I
adjure you by the God of Abraham, I-
faac, and Jacob, that ye flay me not un-
convicted.   If I have wronged any of
you, I am willing to make reftitution to
the utmoft : If I have offended, to fubmit
myfelf, and to implore forgivenefs ; but
O cut me not off in my youth, before I
arrive at the ftate of manhood !" " Yes,
youngfter, replied Simeon, you have
wronged us fo, that you cannot make reftitution.   You have ftolen the affections
of a partial father, which you cannot reftore ; you have fet yourfelf up by your
pretended dreams, as our lord and governor;

ernor; you have made us and our children, yea, and our father himfelf to do
homage to your pride; but we fhall foon
fee what your greatnefs will come to.——
You fhall not live to triumph over your
enflaved brethren: die you muft.".

"Alas! muft I then die for my
dreams! which of you has the government of his fancy whilft afleep. Oh, Simeon! my brother Simeon, could I help
my dreams? I little thought that they
would have given offence to any of
you, when I innocently related them.
I want no fuperiority, I account, myfelf unworthy even of equal regard,
much more fo of fuperior efteem. If
my father fhows any partiality towards
me, it is for my mother's fake, and not
for any thing in me. And muft I die
for any partiality in my father? Make
the cafe your own, my dear Simeon,
would you like to be put to death for
any rovings of your dreaming imagination? To be murdered in cold blood
for what you could not poffibly help?
If I muft die for having dreamed a
dream, which you think portends felicity

city and greatnefs, give me leave to relate to you one that I dreamed laft
night ; if the former excited your anger
and refentment, the latter may as juftly
entitle me to your compaffion and fympathy." Leave obtained, he related
the dream he had in the tent of the
Canaanite, which his brethren heard
with rifing indignation ; and as foon as
he had finifhed, Simeon fpoke to his brethren, with fury flafhing from his eyes ;
" This dream is an artful contrivance
of the infolent wretch to fix a lafting
reproach upon us, and upon our feed;
We, my brethren, are intended by the
deadly ferpents ; perhaps I myfelf am
meant by one of the adders that warped themfelves about his legs, and wak-
ened him in fuch a fright : but why do
we fuffer him to prate any longer ?
One ftroke of my fcymeter will put
an end to his infolence. Ambitious
wretch ! Thou fhalt prate no more."
Here he drew his fword, and rufhed up
to have cloven the ftripling in twain,
but Judah caught him in his arms, and
cried, " Stop, ftop, my Simeon.—Remember

member the promife we have juft now made to Reuben ; wait the time, and let us fee what refolution he comes to."

" O Judah ! cried Jofeph, Judab, my honoured brother ; thou art he whom thy brethren fhall praife : May I hope to find an interceffor in thee ? What if thy fons, either Er or Onan, were in the fame condition in which thou feeft me ? How would thy bowels yearn over them ? See their diftrefs in mine : feel my father's affliction in thine own : act a faithful part in delivering me from mine enraged brethren, who are this day rifen up againft me without a caufe. O Judah, let me owe my life, and all the happinefs of it, to a brother fo honourable in the houfe of his father. And you, O Simeon and Levi think, think of the guilt ye will bring upon yourfelves, by perpetrating a deed fo horrid. Ye may efcape punifhment from the hand of man, but affure yourfelves ye will not efcape from the hand of God. For judgment is his, and he will repay it either in this life, or that which is to come." . Thus

Thus Joſeph interceded for a life, now indeed rendered wretched, by the unkind behaviour of his father's ſons; more out of deſire to diſſuade them from contracting freſh guilt, than from any dread that he had of death, or what ſhould follow after it. Whilſt Reuben retired behind a neighbouring thicket, to pour out the bitterneſs of his ſoul before God, and pray to be directed what part he ſhould act in the preſent iniquitous affair. How ſhall I act ſaid he ? If I conſent, I bring guilt upon my own ſoul and add murder to my inceſt. If I do not conſent, my life is forfeited to the jealouſy of my brethren who will never be eaſy whilſt I am alive, let me be tied to ſecrecy by what oath ſoever. Surrounded by evils, prudence dictates to chuſe the leaſt, that thereby we may eſcape the greater. I muſt at all events endeavor to ſave the boy's life ; in order to which I muſt conſent to his death, and may perhaps win ſo far upon his enemies, as to leave the manner of his death to me. His heart was divided between
the

the thoughts of his own fafety and Jofeph's. The forrow which he forefaw ready to fall upon his aged father, and the guilt juft about to be contracted by his brethren ; but ftill he fteadily determined to ufe his beft endeavors for the fafety of the youth. With this refolution, although diffembled, he returned to the reft feemingly with a placid countenance ; and thus addreffed them. My brethren, I am now ready to concur with your meafures, and even to be active therein, upon one fmall condition being granted me, which is, that inftead of fhedding of his blood, we confine him till death in yonder pit, on the other fide of the pafture." Agreed, replied his brethren: So that he dies, no matter how. And hereby Reuben makes himfelf not only an accomplice, but a principal actor in the tragedy. Away with him to the pit, and there let the fun, moon, and ftars, pay their court to him as their governor."

At this inftant, they hurried him away to the propofed pit, whilft he in

anguifh

anguish of heart, summoned them all to meet him hereafter before the judgment seat of the King of Kings, where, he assured them he should have justice done him. This appeal he designed as a means of conviction, whereby his brethren might be brought to repentance that their sins might be blotted out, when times of refreshing should come from the presence of the Lord.

Joseph, now let down into the pit; Reuben rejoiced in hope of having it in his power to deliver him safe the ensuing night to his good old father; whose heart he knew must pant with painful anxiety till his return. Having determined upon this salutary project, he left him there and went to dispatch some pastoral business among the menial herdsmen, at a different part of the wilderness, proposing ere long to return. In the mean while, Joseph having nothing but death to expect, and hardly even desiring any thing else, lift up his soul in fervent prayer to the God of his salvation. " Thou God," he cried, " whose presence fills immensity itself, whose eyes see, and
whose

whose eye-lids try the actions and hearts
of men ; thou muſt of neceſſity be preſent here, and witneſs to all my treatment from my brethren.   So far as the
appointment is thine, I deſire cheerfully
to ſubmit to it, and own thy conduct
juſt, as I have deſerved a thouſand
deaths ere now. But Lord, my brethren's motives differ from thine as far as
eaſt from weſt, for envy do they now
riſe up againſt me.   Here I am in all
appearance ſhut up for certain death..
My God, let not my blood be charged
upon the ſons of my father. My God
forgive their iniquity. And O Lord
do thou ſupport my aged father under
the pangs of ſorrow, which he will from
his paternal fondneſs neceſſarily feel.
Support him, O my God, and give him
to bear his affliction in my loſs, becoming the parent of the choſen race. Here
I am, thou God of heaven and earth.——
I muſt die if thou interpoſeſt not. If
death is deſigned for me, help me to
bear it with humble reſignation ; but
Lord, if thou pleaſeſt to prolong a life
altogether inſignificant, thou haſt the
means

means in thine own hand.. Ufe them as
will be moft for thy glory." Here he
was furprifed by an uncommon radiance
which diffufed itfelf through the place..
A fplendor which overcame him with-
the fweeteft fenfation, and gave his en-
raptured foul a large tafte of ethereal
felicity. The amazing brightnefs a little diminifhed, fo far as to enable mor-
tal eyes to endure it, there ftood a
blooming youth confeft to his view.——
The inftant the celeftial vifitant difcovered himfelf, he thus accofted the fon of
Jacob. " I am fent, by my God and
thine am I fent, to inform thee that he
is well acquainted with all thy afflictions
and perfectly knows thy prefent diftrefs.
Not Jehovah only, but the hofts of heaven, in general are witneffes of thy mi-
fery. The celeftial legions bowed over
the brow of heaven, and beheld the
baleful deed with as much uneafinefs
and fearful apprehenfions for thee, as celeftial fpirits are capable of, till the purpofe of the Eternal was revealed. But
this calmed every mind, and the fover-
eign will of thy God, reconciled in an
inftant.

inftant the will of miriads.   I am Abel
the proto-martyr.   I fell, my Jofeph,
by the hand of my brother Cain, and
the **day** of my fall was the day of my
exaltation.   O Jofeph, did you but
know the joys prepared for thofe that
love the Lord, you would not wifh to
prolong life a moment.   But your time
is not come.   You are defigned to fof-
ter infant Ifrael under the fhadow of
your wings.   You muft be fold into E-
gypt to govern that fertile land, and provide fuftenance for the feed of the promife.   Even to day you muft be gone,
for thy God makes ufe of thy brethrens'
jealoufy for this very purpofe.   Only remember that when thou art in Egypt
thou wilt be tempted, but keep it ever
in thy mind that the God of the Hebrews fent thee thither.   There fhall
thy brethren bow down to thee.   There
fhalt thou embrace thy father, and there
fhall Benjamin fall upon thy neck and
fhed the fraternal tear.   Be not careful
about thy father's affliction.   Leave him
to his God, he fhall be fupported and
brought through.   When the day is
                                    thine

thine think well of thy brother Reuben,
he had thee here purpofely to deliver
thee, but he muft fee thee no more, till
you meet in the court of Pharoah.   I
leave thee Jofeph, the peace of thy God
go with thee.

THE

THE

LIFE

OF

JOSEPH.

E

ARGUMENT.

Joseph taken out of the pit—Sold to Alvah
an Ishmaelite--Reuben returns to the pit—
His sorrow & despair on missing Joseph—
His lamentation—He chargeth the murder upon his brethren—Judah repents of
what was done and informs Reuben—
They send out messengers to overtake him
and bring him back—An angel appears
to Reuben and comforts him—They dip
Joseph's coat in blood and send it to Jacob
—Jacob's grief and Dinah's despair—
Joseph's arrival in Egypt—The friendly
treatment he meets with from Alvah—
He chooseth to abide in Egypt—Potiphar
sees him on the mart and conceives a liking
to him—Purchases him and presents him
to Sabrina his new married lady—A
grand hunting match in the desart—Joseph kills a lion and delivers his mistress—
Sabrina conceives a violent passion for
him—Gabriel inspires Joseph with a
dream ominous of danger—His prosperity
—Joseph saves his mistress a second time
from a band of Arabs—His mistress's
passion thereby greatly inflamed.

BOOK II.

ABSORBED in thought the fon of Ifrael lay, after the heavenly vifion was departed, when Judah came to the brim of the pit, and calling Jofeph by name, let down a rope which he ordered him to tie about his body below his arms, then he and his brethren drew him out of the pit, and led him to a numerous caravan of merchants, going from Gilead to Egypt, with myrrh, balm, and fpicery. Confident in the word of the heavenly meffenger he afcended out of the pit dreading no evil, and fuffered himfelf to be fold to Alvah, the chief of the company for twenty pieces of filver. The youthful beauty and mature understanding of our hero, equally confpired to endear him to his mafter, who foon employed him in the
government

government of his camels, with whom we leave him whilst we follow Reuben from the distant field to the pit. "Joseph, my brother Joseph," he cried, but Joseph made no answer, he repeated the doleful invitation, but still no voice was heard. He rent his garments, tore his hair, and roamed about the brink of the pit in the greatest anguish of soul, almost to throw himself down into it, and die with his lost brother. At last having spent himself to no purpose, he called Joseph's last dream to remembrance, and dreaded its being literally fulfiled. Then he thought again, can my brethren have treacherously murdered him in the absence of his friend. O. false and dreadful brethren ! cruel and bloody men ! to shed the blood of the innocent, contrary to solemn contract. Racked with despair and glowing resentment, he reasoned within himself, whether it were not best to rush upon his brethren and plunge his dagger in each of their hearts, one by one, till he himself should perish upon the points of their swords. In one

minute

minute he was fully bent upon the bloody purpose, in the next, the horrors of an agonizing parent expiring over his murdered family, pierced him to the heart. Then he cried, " O my father, my father, how wretchedly am I deceived ? I thought to have been happy in making some atonement for my paft guilt, by delivering thy darling from his murderous brethren, and reftoring him fafe to thy fond embrace. But, ah ! I am deceived. Jofeph is loft, irretrieveably loft. And what forrows will wring the heart of my parent, when he learns that Jofeph is no more. O my Jofeph, gladly would I revenge thy blood upon thy murderers. But, alas ! the lofs of one is more than enough for a tender parent to bear. How would his aged heart fink under the carnage which this arm would make, fhould I give fcope to my juft revenge ? But, O my father, my father, for thy fake I live, and leave it to God to avenge the death of thy fon. So faying, he went up to his brethren, grief and refentment fparkling in his eyes."

" Falfe

" Falfe men, where is the lad ? Where is Jofeph ? Could you not withhold your bloody hand from him for one night, that the unhappy youth might have had time to pour out his heart unto his God ? But alas ! he is gone. And I, whither fhall I fly ? How fhall I anfwer to his father for his untimely death ? What agonies muft the good man feel, when he hears that Jofeph is no more ? O my father ! O Jofeph ! my poor Jofeph." So faying, his over fwelled heart breaks forth in gufhing forrow, which trickled down his manly cheeks like chriftial waters from the diamond rock. But furely never did tears better become the mafculine countenance than now ! Such was the anguifh of Reuben's fpirit, that like a contagion, his grief reached the hearts of his brethren : and even Simeon himfelf, felt for a moment fomething like remorfe. A folemn filence reigned in the whofe affembly.

Judah at laft broke through the gloom that covered them, and addreffed Reuben. " My brother, permit your forrow to fubfide, fuffer your rea-

fon

fon to fupercede your paffion, and cool-
ly hear what I have to offer.. I am
now thoroughly convinced that what
we have done is wrong, notwithftanding Jofeph is yet alive." Reuben
quckly replied, " If he lives let me fet
my eyes upon him that my heart may
be at reft." " Alas, faid Judah, though
he lives, I cannot prefent him to you.
For I, even I, to fave his life, advifed
to fell him to fome Midianitifh merchants, who paffed by here in your abfence. This is done and cannot be undone, or it fhould. And I am now
more convinced than ever that he will
live to fee his dreams fulfilled, and his
brethren to bow down unto him. Yes,
my brethren, his laft night's dream has
been amply verified, for it may be truly faid, he fell into a pit of ferpents,
even in the houfe of his father. I feel
within me fome monitor telling me,
that God who weighs the actions of
men in an even balance, will vifit and
punifh my having concurred in feparat-
ing Jofeph from his father and brethren,
by the judicial death of my own children

dren.   O that it was undone again, and
that we had it in our power to reſtore
him to his father."

All the brethren heartily concurred
in Judah's ſentiments, Simeon alone
excepted, " For his part, he ſaid, all
that he grieved at, was, that they had
ſuffered him to eſcape, and leave him
within the poſſibility of ſuperiority.——
When we had him, ſaid he, it was
madneſs to let him go." " I would
not for the world, ſaid the reſt of his
brethren, Simeon, that it had been as
you would have wiſhed it." But Reuben, flew from his place like light--
ning, and would inſtantly have killed
Simeon ; but that Napthali, who perceived from his countenance, the effect
that Simeon's ſanguinary ſpeech had
made upon his heart, aroſe with the
ſwiftneſs of a hind ; caught his elder
brother by the arm, and begged for
Jacob's ſake that he would moderate
his paſſion.   Again compoſed, the brethren conſult how they may ſtrive to regain their loſt brother.   It was agreed
to ſend out meſſengers early in the
                                     morning

morning, to overtake the Ishmaelites, offer to Alvah the price given for Joseph, and as much more as might procure his release. This agreed upon, and messengers appointed for the negociation, they all retired to rest, every one with his servants to his separate tent. Reuben was just laid down, and striving to compose himself to rest, when a dazzling glory shone through all the tent, and a voice more than human, called him by name, " Reuben, Reuben, first born of Israel, hear my words and attend unto my speech.— You mourn for Joseph, and not without cause, considering the occasion of his exile. But know this, that he is the peculiar care of his God, who is with him wherever he goes, and who will make whatever he does to prosper.— He shall find a friend, a father, and brethren in a strange land, where he shall dwell securely, till his brethren, unknown to themselves, shall bow down unto him with the humblest supplications. For Joseph shall be found.— Thine arms shall yet embrace him, Reuben,

ben.' And the whole world fhall know him as the nurfing father of the chofen race. Meanwhile, fecure thine own life, Reuben, by concealing the matter from hoary Ifrael, left the rage of thy brethren mix thee untimely with the duft ; for fome of them are old in bloodfhed, and fhudder not at human carnage. Obferve my words and all fhall be well."

As Phœbus approached the north-eaft verge of this dufky world, and fair Aurora purpled the fky, the meffengers fet out by different ways; to overtake the caravan, they roamed through howling waftes and fandy defarts to no purpofe, till fpent with the fatigue of the day; they returned faint and weary on the enfuing night, to their brethren at Dothan. Every countenance difcovered difguft and forrow ; even Simeon could have wifhed for Jofeph's return. Reuben alone maintained a placid countenance, to the furprife of all his brethren who faw his rage and defpair fo fuddenly turned into calm ferenity. He faid, " Come, my brethren, let us

leave

leave of caring for Joseph. The pious youth is the care of his God, who will never forsake the needy in their affliction. Let us concert some measures to support our good old father under the heavy weight of affliction, just falling upon his venerable head. O Jacob! revered old man, my heart bleeds for thee. A tide of sorrow will soon overwhelm thee. But thou hast the promise, and thy God is thine. May he indeed be near to thee."

Matters being as they are, said Asher, I hold it good that we kill a kid or a lamb, take Joseph's many coloured coat, rend it in divers places, and smear it with the blood of the slain beast, and send it to our father, who will naturally conclude, that some hungry lion has devoured him, and we his sons shall be freed from all suspicion. We are necessitated either to confess the fact, or cover it over with dissimulation. If we do the former, we draw down the curse of our father upon us, and there is at least a strong probability, that by the latter we shall retain his love and confidence :

dence : though God knows we little deferve it."

The advice given by Afher, was immediately approved, and Simeon and Levi, were appointed the meffengers to carry the coat unto Jacob, all the reft being unable to bear the forrow of their parent upon this mournful occafion.—— How nearly allied is one fin to another? The fons of Jacob have now no covering for their infamy, but lying and diffimulation. "Welcome my fons, welcome Simeon and Levi, fays the tender patriarch, how do all your brethren my children, and how does Jofeph?" "Our brethren, Sir, are all well, but as for Jofeph we have feen nothing of him."—— "Seen nothing of him ! replied he, thefe five days are gone fince I fent him forth to vifit his brethren, and enquire after your health. I pray God, that my fears may be groundlefs. O that no harm may have befallen my boy !" We would hope for the beft, Sir, and yet we are not without fear about him ourfelves, faid they, feeing he is not at home. As we came along through the wildernefs,

wilderness, we found a coat that somewhat resembles our brother's, but you
will better judge of it when you see it.
This, Sir, is the coat we found ; see
now whether it be thy son's coat or not."
"Ah ! it is my son's coat indeed. Without doubt Joseph is torn to pieces," he
said, and the blood receding from his
countenance, he sunk down into the
chair, and could not for a long time be
recovered from his fit.   The houshold
was alarmed.   Benjamin and all his
daughters flew to his affistance, and the
general cry was—O our father ! Our
father ! Our good father is dying.   Dinah flew about the tent, tearing her hair
in the utmoft diftraction, crying, "O my
father, my father, would to God I had
died in thy ftead.   What shall thy
daughter, thy friendlefs Dinah do now?
A dishonor to her race ; now turned
out into an inhofpitable world, without
the protection of a father.   Wretched
Dinah ! Better thou hadft never been
born ! Curfed be the fon of Hamor.—
Curfed be he that glories in the deftruction of a virgin."   One of the female

train

train chafed his withered limbs, another rubbed his temples with odours, till at laft life began to return. Fetching a deep figh.   His eyes widely rolling, he afked, " Where am I ? What has been the matter my daughters? Why have ye difturbed me ? I am now awakened from the foundeft fleep that ever I fell into. My Dinah, where is fhe ? Tell me my girl what ails thee ? I am thy father, Dinah.; come near my love, and let me embrace thee.   Bid Jofeph to come fpeedily, I want to fee him.   Ay, now I have hit the fore.   Jofeph is gone, Dinah ! Jofeph is rent to pieces.   Bring that bloody coat.   That coat, Benjamin, is thy brother Jofeph's.   He wears it no more..   Some of that voracious army, wherewithal God hath plagued finful man, hath torn him in pieces and devoured him.   O my Jofeph ! my Jofeph ! Had I a thoufand lives, I would have given them all to have redeemed thee from death.   But thou art gone my fon, forever gone from the land of light, and I fhall foon follow , thee into that of darknefs.   I come my fon.

son. I follow thee, I soon shall join thee
in the land afar off. Hasten thy pace
thou tardy executioner ; cut short thy
work thou friendly enemy ; I long once
more to encircle my son in thefe withered arms. Yet my Dinah, poor ruin-
ed damfel, if I could, I would live for
thy fake, a little to alleviate thy forrows.
But I die my girl ; I find I cannot long
furvive my Jofeph." Lovely Benjamin, Dinah, and their fifters endeavor-
ed to confole the mourning patriarch
under his heavy lofs. But all in vain.
He refufed to be comforted, faying,
" Nay, but I will die with my fon."
Shunah the wife of Judah, Tamah the
wife of Simeon, and Zillah the wife of
Napthali, endeavoured to fet before
him his numerous feed. His eleven
remaining fons, their prefent offspring,
and the profpect of a numerous iffue.
But the good man replied, " Thefe are
not my Jofeph," and funk into another
fit of agonizing forrow. Thus he giev-
ed from day to day for the lofs of his
fon, nor could all the endeavours of
his children comfort him.

Jofeph

Joseph and his company drew near to Memphis, the capital of Egypt, where the merchants intended to dispose of their goods. And here Alvah the Ishmael-ite, found a market for his young He-brew likewise. Alvah had seen so much of Joseph's dexterity in the ma-nagement of his affairs, and was so de-lighted with his piety and good sense, that he would gladly have kept him for his own servant, had it been his pleasure to have continued with him ; but know-ing his distressed circumstances, deem-ed it ungenerous to lay any constraint upon his inclination.

Therefore the evening after their arrival in Memphis, he calleth Joseph to him, and thus addressed him. " My young man, I am perfectly sensible that for envy you was separated from your father's house, and sold unto me. Since you came under my direction, your agreeable converse, your courte-ous and affable conduct, has perfectly gained my affections. If you are con-tent to abide with me, I will use you as a friend rather than a servant ; for

you

you are dear to me Joseph, as if you was my own fon. Neverthelefs as you may have your objections to returning to the land where your barbarous brethren refide, and as I am uninformed concerning the purpofes of your God towards you, I leave you to your own voluntary choice, either to return with me, or to abide in Egypt.. But if you fix upon Egypt as your refidence, you muft be fold my Joseph—Sold as a flave my friend, notwithftanding I believe you are born to rule." The fon of Jacob refpectfully replied. "My dear Sir, my honoured Alvah, my friend, my father, permit me to call you by that endearing name ;.I cannot enough admire the goodnefs of God who provides for me in ftrangers, that friendfhip which was denied me in the houfe of my brethren. All was cruelty from them, but friendfhip my dear mafter has run through the whole of your conduct towards me. Inclination, Sir, would induce me to follow your fortune good or bad, but a fecret meffage delivered to me by an heavenly meffenger not

two

two hours before I was fold unto you,
obliges me, as your will coincides there-
with, to abide a bondman in Egypt.—
I would not as yet willingly divulge
the contents of the meffage referred to ;
but the time will come my honoured
mafter, that I fhall more fully reveal
the caufe of my banifhment.   Then
you will clearly fee that want of refpect
to you is no part of the reafon why I
defire to leave your very agreeable fervice.   Permit me, Sir, to beg your en-
deavour to difpofe of me as you would
wifh to have your own fon difpofed of
in fimilar circumftances, and let me
owe my good fortune, if fuch fhould
befal me in a ftrange land, to a man to
whom I am already under fo many great
obligations.   Thus, Sir, will you bind
me to you for ever, and make me more
yours than I poffibly could be as one of
your domeftic fervants."

  " I will Jofeph, replied the good Ifhmaelite, I will take care to difpofe of
you to your beft advantage.   I will be
to you in place of a father at this time.
But when you are advanced my fon,
                              as

as God, even the God of your father
Abraham will advance you to the high-
eft honours, forget not your friend.——
Think of poor Alvah, and for my fake
deal favourably with my feed, fhould,
they ever make fupplication unto you.
I will enhance your price my friend,
in fome low proportion to your worth,,
but not a penny of it fhall abide with
me, for I have profited greatly by your
prefence already." "My dear Sir, replied Jofeph, you are a merchant, and
muft live upon your gain, why fhould
you throw away any part of it upon a
poor unworthy ftranger?" "I tell you
Jofeph, returned he with fome emotion,
you are a friend of the Almighty's, and
your God will never let poor Alvah
be a lofer by any little kindnefs which
he may fhew to you. Be fatisfied Jofeph. Be content I fay. And prepare
yourfelf by to-morrow noon for the
market, and here, let me fee, take thefe
few pieces to provide yourfelf with decent appa███ ; and I in the mean while,
will be ██king what meafures I can for
your good." So faying he turned and
gave

gave no time for reply. Joseph overwhelmed with gratitude, burst forth into tears, admiring the wisdom and goodness of God in raising up unto him, as
it were a second Jacob in the person of
Alvah. "O thou Holy one, he cried,
I am now convinced of thine omnipre-
sence and superintendency over human
affairs. I admire thy wisdom, I adore
thy goodness to me, who am unworthy
of the least of all thy mercies; go on
my God to perfect what thou hast begun, and succeed the earnest endeavours of benevolent Alvah, in my be-
half, and succeed thou me, and be thou
with me, my father and my friend, in
this land wherein I am a stranger, and
the glory of all will ultimately redound
unto thee. Amen."

The time arrived that Joseph must
appear for sale, he came arrayed in
plain, but decent apparel, which shewed
the graces of his person to the best advantage. His master and he had but
just come to the mart, when Potiphar,
a renowned officer in the army, and
captain general of the forces of Egypt,
happened

happened to come paſt, and fixing his eye upon him, conceived a ſingular liking for him. What pity is it, ſaid he within himſelf, to ſee a perſon of ſuch an attractive deportment, diſplaying a countenance ſo diſtinguiſhingly lovely, expoſed to ſale to every ſordid wretch of a maſter ? If money will redeem him from ſlavery, it ſhall be done, and I think I ſhall deem myſelf happy in having releaſed one of the moſt amiable of human kind. " What is the price of this young man, my maſter ?"

" If he is ſold, Sir, replied Alvah, an hundred and fifty pieces is his price ; but I ſell him not, unleſs I know to whom, and what treatment he is likely to meet with. For it is not neceſſity, but choice that detains him in Egypt." " My name, ſaid he, is Potiphar, I am of ſome conſideration in the ſtate, and near the perſon of his majeſty." " Then Sir, the young man is yours at your own price, and I hope you will conſider him as one that might have expected better fortunes, but for the malice and envy of jealous brethren. I

am

am proud, Sir, to recommend him to
you as the moſt virtuous, faithful, and
pious of his race." It is agreed. "Are
you willing to follow the fortune of Potiphar?" " I am willing to be his humble
ſervant, if Sir, you are he." " Here then
merchant, here is your money." "One
word Sir, ere the bargain is cloſed, and
that is, that as I trade to this place, I
muſt beg leave to have a friendly inter--
view occaſionally with my friend Jóſeph,
for he is my friend; although I have the
power of diſpoſing of him at preſent."
" Far be it from Potiphar to hinder the
youth he loves from acceſs to his friends.
You are welcome at all times to viſit
your youthful, your amiable friend."

Joſeph was placed in Potiphar's family, after Alvah had according to pro-
miſe, obliged him to accept of the hundred and fifty pieces, for which he was
ſold, and taken a tender farewel of him
for a ſeaſon. He had not been long in
his new ſtation before he gave ſuch
proofs of his probity, as gained him the
eſteem of all the family.

Potiphar was but lately married to a
beautiful

beautiful lady of the firft rank, whofe
name was Sabrina; given to the captain by his majefty himfelf. The better to folemnize the nuptials of his warlike officer, the king appointed an hunting match in the defart of Arabia,
where he was gracioufly pleafed himfelf to attend Potiphar and Sabrina.——
They had not long ranged the lonely
wild, ere they roufed a monftrous lion,
mafter of a favage family, at whofe appearance even the hardeft of them gave
back. The furly monfter with furious
difdain flafhing from his eyes, ftalked
flow in fullen majefty, and with eyes
afkance furveyed his competitors, till
perceiving himfelf overmatched by the
number of baying hounds, juft letting
loofe upon him, he took to his heels,
and fought refuge in the diftant thicket.
Sabrina, mounted on a fwift Arabian
horfe, well accuftomed to exercifes of
this kind, furpaffed the hounds, and
even outfled the wind; expofed herfelf
to the greateft danger, to the terror of
the noble company, none of whom
could come near her, Jofeph alone excepted

cepted. Mounted on the fleeteft of his mafter's courfers, he kept clofe to his lady; and well for her it was fo; for coming to the edge, of the thicket, which by reafon of its clofenefs, would not admit the entrance of the lion; who finding himfelf fo clofely purfued, turned fiercely upon his enemies. Sabrina being next unto him, had no doubt fallen a prey to his fury, had not Jofeph rufhed between her and danger. The favage roared like the loudeft thunder and flew in the greateft ferocity at the lady, who almoft fwooned with the fright, whilft Jofeph fprung from his horfe, goared the monfter in the neck, and pinned him faft with his fpear to the earth. By this time Potiphar himfelf arrived, and ftruck with aftonifhment, partly at the danger in which his Sabrina had been, and partly at the heroic fortitude of his new and beloved fervant, he could not fpeak a word, till falling firft on the bofom of his fpoufe, a..d then upon Jofeph's neck, he poured forth a flood of joy and gratitude. He inftantly enfranchifed the

deliverer

deliverer of his love and placed him at the head of his family, where he acted in all respects as one who serveth not man so much as God. Such circumspection and fidelity rarely attend the stewards of gentlemen of elevated rank. Joseph was exceeding lovely in his person, and the late instance of his gallantry and fortitude, made a criminal impression on the mind of his lady, whilst he unsuspecting thereof, from a principle of duty and benevolence, performed both to her and to his lord, all the good offices within his power, which altho' a duty incumbent on him, contributed to foster the latent flame unlawfully kindled in her warped heart.

The Almighty Jehovah, whose all-seeing eye, with one comprehensive glance, examineth all our thoughts, whether virtuous or corrupt ; seeing the workings of Sabrina's heart, and having destined the blooming youth to escape the snare so fatal to his hopes, as well as ruinous to the peace of his undisturbed mind, commanded Gabriel to descend to earth, and give the stripling some

G striking

striking imitation of the danger he was in, yet still to conceal the quarter from whence it was to come. Obedient to the high behest of the Eternal, the seraph prest with glowing ardour, binds on his golden pinions, shoots through the vault of ether, and stops not till arrived at the palace of Potiphar, when gloomy night in her ebon car had measured half her lonesome journey. He breathed an odoriferous gale upon the bed, and instantly the Hebrew exile, felt the warm glow of exalted virtue, ascending towards the empyreum.—— Sweet was the slumber when the pious soul breathed after joys of an immortal nature. Soon he fancied himself, studious of his master's affairs, assiduously promoting the interest of his generous patron. Thus employed, he saw an hand drawing a net composed of golden wire around the place where he stood, and instantly found himself intangled therein. The snare appeared so formidable, that he saw no way of escape left for him, nor could he tell to what purpose he was thus involved. Consider-

ing

ing himself as a prisoner in this golden
snare, he heard a voice as it had been
from the aerial regions. " O Joseph !
most favoured of the children of Jacob;
remember thou the God of the Hebrews.
Take hold of the strength of Omnipo-
tence, and one vigorous effort, delivers
thee from the snare." This said, the
young patriarch lift up his heart to his
God, in this short ejaculation. "O God
of my fathers, Abraham, Isaac & Jacob,
for the sake of him who shall bruise the
serpent's head, and destroy the snare of
the devil, assist me this once and deliver
me." Then collecting all his force, he
exerted himself in one vigorous struggle,
and found the wires break as easily, as
Sampson afterwards did the new cords
with which he was bound. Just as he
sprung into liberty, he awoke and rejoiced that it was but a dream.

Joseph's God was with him in whatever he did. He gave him singular
wisdom and prudence in the management of all his affairs, insomuch, that
whatever he did prospered in his hands ;
which led his lord to rely upon his wis-

dom

dom and integrity, with a perfect con--
fidence ; and unrefervedly commit unto his care, the fole management of all
his ftate.   Unenvied, he enjoyed this
flow of calm profperity, without any
mixture of bitternefs, befides that which
arofe from his banifhment from Jacob
and Benjamin.   Happy had it been for
Sabrina, if her heart had been as free
from unlawful defire as was that of her
amiable Hebrew.   But alas ! fhe fondly
encouraged the pleafing wifh, till it arofe
to a paffion too ftrong for her to fubdue.
Shame induced her long to conceal the
guilty flame, yet in fpite of art and ftu-
dious care, an inward langour difcovered
itfelf in the penfivenefs of her countenance.   Her unfufpecting lord, called
every poffible means to her affiftance.
The fons of Efculapius exhaufted their
fkill ; the whole Materia Medica was
ranfacked for a cure, every diverfion
which pleafantry could devife, in vain
was inftituted to divert the gloom of her
folitary mind.   She was never happy in
any diverfion, unlefs Jofeph made one of
the party.   Her only feafons of plea-
                                    fure

sure were when she could prevail with
him to fit with her, and entertain her
with the history of his native country ;
which he, unskilled in the mysteries of
love, very readily consented to.

About this time an accident happened, which served greatly to increase the
fatal passion. Potiphar & Sabrina went
on a visit to Ira, a Lybian prince, where
they plenteously enjoyed the rites of hof-
pitality for two or three weeks, but un-
happily were attacked by a band of Arabs
as they repassed the howling wilderness.
At the first discovery of them, Sabrina
sunk as a person dying in the arms of her
husband, and her soul stood as it were
on tiptoe, on her pale trembling lip.
As a panther rusheth from the thicket,
to seize the passing prey, Joseph bound-
ed from the chariot, vaulted on a led
horse, and encouraged the menials to
stand by their noble patrons. The Arabs
charged them with resolution and vigor ;
animated by the intrepidity of our hero,
the Egyptians returned the charge, and
sent amongst them a score of winged
deaths, every arrow marked by fate.——

G 2   Then

Then Joseph putting spurs to his horse, rode up to the enemy, and with his sabre divided the head of Mezero, their captain, from his body, and dealt death to many of the Arabs : the servants of Potiphar, following the example of their leader, above half the banditti were presently dispatched, whilst the rest sought to hide themselves from death by flight. Joseph pursued and killed many more, as they strove to fly from his avenging arm. Sabrina being somewhat recovered, Potiphar himself flew to the assistance of his guard, fierce as the lion ravaging for prey ; but the work was done, and the enemy discomfited ere he could arrive. Sabrina from the charriot beheld the heroic fortitude of the gallant Hebrew, as he raged along the ranks of the enemy, and every wound he inflicted upon them, was as oil poured into the latent flame.

The grateful soul of the young patriarch rejoiced at having it in his power to manifest the sense which he had of their goodness, by exerting himself in their defence, in a season of difficulty
and

and danger. With modesty he received Potiphar's caresses, who presented him to his lady as her friend and deliverer. His address to his mistress, was full of duty, gratitude and affection. All which encouraged her to hope, that he was smote with the same guilty passion with herself, and made her half resolve at a time convenient, to come to an avowal. Again she resolved to wait yet farther, to see whether his confession, would save her from that confusion.

THE

THE

LIFE

OF

JOSEPH.

ARGUMENT.

*Syrena comforts her miſtreſs, by promiſing ſuc-
ceſs to her amour—She ſtrives to entice him
—in vain—She perſuades her lady to an
avowal—His miſtreſs confeſſeth her love
—Solicits his embrace— To divert her
attention from it, he relates the ſtory of
Eve eating the forbidden fruit—Applies
it to his miſtreſs, with a view to reani-
mate her virtue—He relates his ſiſter's
raviſhment, and its fatal conſequences—
Her ſilence and diſcontent at his coldneſs—
Conſults her nurſe, who encourageth her
to perſiſt—She commandeth Joſeph to her
chamber—Strives to win him by perſua-
ſion—Then to force him—He flies from
her, and leaves his ſcarf behind—Her
love turns to rage and hatred—She ac-
cuſeth him of an attempt upon her honor—
He is impriſoned.*

BOOK III.

SYRENA, a person well skilled in all the wily mazes of woman kind, was governess to Sabrina, in her virgin years, and now attended her in the capacity of waiting woman. She alone was instructed with the fatal secret ; her mistress having had full proof of her readiness to concur in any measures to gratify her inclination. She consoled her distress and flattered her passion, by assuring her, that as far as she could dive into the secrets of a youthful heart, Joseph was glowing with a passion, at least equal to her own. She could read it well in his looks and in his sighs ; for amidst all his prosperity Joseph could not help sighing after his guilty brethren, and his distressed honourable father, from whose embraces he

was

was baniſhed without a cauſe. She promiſed to uſe all her wiſdom to ſerve her miſtreſs, and did not doubt by her prudent management to bring the blooming Hebrew to her fond embraces. As he was one day in his office ſettling his maſter's accounts, Syrena entered, and having ſhut the door, ſhe thus accoſted him. " Maſter Joſeph, be idle who will, we are always ſure to find you in your buſineſs. Indeed maſter Joſeph our lord is happy in having ſuch a ſervant as yourſelf. I do not wonder that both he and my lady have ſuch an high eſteem for you." "'I tell you Mrs. Syrena, replied Joſeph, I do nothing but what is my duty. My honourable maſter and lady have a right to my beſt ſervices, and I ſhould be ſhamefully wanting in my duty to God, to them, and myſelf, if I did not ſtudy to my utmoſt to promote their honour, advantage and delight." "I am glad, Sir, replied Syrena, that your virtuous ſentiments concur ſo exactly with my own. And I can tell you, Mr. Joſeph, that more tenderneſs is due from you to

your

your amiable miſtreſs, than perhaps you are aware of." " I know ſaid he, that my lady is amiable and virtuous, and merits my humbleſt regard, which I ſhall ever be ready to render her with the utmoſt pleaſure." " She is virtuous, ſaid Syrena, and yet I can tell you Joſeph, ſhe cannot help being ſenſible of your attractions, and entertaining the fondneſs of affection for you. I wrung the painful ſecret with the greateſt difficulty from her lips. And you my friend may avail yourſelf of your happineſs, and embrace a favour which ſhe would deny to any but yourſelf, was he even the firſt prince of the blood." Rejoined the patriarch, " My maſter and miſtreſs are daily loading me with favours, of which I am altogether unworthy. I believe their readineſs to add more as occaſion may offer. But the lips that would inſinuate ſo much as an hint contrary to my miſtreſs's honor, ought to be ſealed in everlaſting ſilence." "Not ſo faſt, Sir, returned ſhe, I tell you ſhe loves you, and longs for your embrace. But I enjoin you to conceal the fatal

H ‘truth,

truth, and improve it to your own advantage." She ended here, and returned to her lady, who waited impatiently the iſſue of this converſation.

Syrena failed not to enlarge upon her own ſagacity and addreſs, ſhe related the converſe ſhe had had with Joſeph, in the manner which would beſt flatter her lady's paſſion; and from the whole ſhe inferred that it was caution in the Hebrew, which cauſed him to feign ignorance. But ſhe was ſure that amidſt all his care to conceal it, ſhe could diſcern flaſhes of paſſion dart from his amorous eye, when the name of Sabrina was mentioned. In ſhort, Madam, continued ſhe, the matter muſt be between you and him, for I perceive he is ſo cautious, that he will admit none into the ſecret beſide yourſelves. And indeed I cannot blame him when I conſider how falſe and deceitful the greater part of people are. You know Madam, he is young, and a ſtranger to intercourſe with our ſex; and who knows how far modeſty may keep him back from an avowal; beſides he may
fear

fear your ladyship's refentment in cafe your paffion fhould not be anfwerable to his."

" O Syrena ! replied the wife of Potiphar, thou knoweft that in our fex an avowal is hard, even when the object is lawful ; but how much more fo muft it be when the object is criminal, and an avowal is the difplay of our guilt and fhame. Yet I would even venture to confefs my love to him, could I but hope the haughty youth would embrace my propofal. But, O Syrena, fhould he refufe it, then fhould I be undone. His perfon is amiable and lovely, his conduct affable and polite, his fpirit open and benevolent ; but his virtue, Syrena ! I fear his virtue is inflexible."
" O Madam, replied the fwarthy Duenna; no virtue can be proof againft fuch charms as yours. The Hebrew will fall an eafy victim, when he is affured of your affection."

Encouraged by the affurances of Syrena, fhe refolves to abandon fhame and modefty at once, and folicit Jofeph to her embrace. To this purpofe fhe
propofes

propofes an airing, and requires him to attend her in Potiphar's abfence, in her chariot. As they were on the way with a fcarlet blufh upon her countenance, and defire fparkling in her eyes, with a faultring voice that befpoke the blacknefs of her guilt, fhe faid, " Jofeph you cannot be ignorant of my defire for your company, and yet I can tell you, that if your bofom is proof againft love, love even to me, I may rue the day that ever I beheld your too amiable face. For I love you Jofeph ; my pain forces me to confefs my fhame, I have trufted my honour in your hand, I hope you will act with your ufual gallantry." She faid, then leaning her head on his fnowy bofom, melted into a flood of tears, which fhe endeavoured but in vain to conceal. Aftonifhed at this open declaration, it was fometime before he was capable of fpeech or reflection.

After a long filence, accompanied with tears upon her part, and heartfelt fighs upon his, not without ftruggles between corruption and virtue, in broken

ken accents he replied : " Your honour, my lady, is ever safe with your
unworthy servant, whose greatest glory
is to be faithful to the trust reposed in
him. But before I explain myself upon this matter, will your ladyship give
me leave to relate an affair which is
better known among the children of
Shem, than among the descendants of
Ham. After leave obtained, with hope
of extricaing himself from his present
difficulty, and working some suitable
impression upon the mind of his mistress, he thus begun.

" When our first parents Adam and
Eve originally dropped from the all-
forming hand, they were perfectly free
from any bias to evil ; not one corrupt inclination possessed their peaceful
breasts. This calm serenity, this sweet
composure, continued with them as
long as they retained their innocence.
But to their sad experience they ere
long found that the effect of guilt is dire
alarm and incessant perturbation. Our
benevolent Creator was pleased to put
the parents of mandkind in possession of

the paradifaical garden, where a perpet-
ual fpring cheered the bleffed mound,
and every falubrious vegetable. All
that thine eyes behold, all that the earth
produceth, Adam, is thine, faith the
munificent Deity. I give thee leave
to ufe thy utmoft freedom with all the
produce of the earth. One tree, and
only one I forbid thee to touch. Its,
fertile boughs indeed bend low beneath
its fruit, which pendant ha~~ng~~ attractive
of the eye. This Adam, is the forbidden tree. Thefe are the fruit, to tafte
of which, is death. Beware of it man,
come not near it Adam, for on the day
thou eateft of it, thou fhalt furely die.
Incautious Eve, the mother of humanity, in an evil hour was prevailed upon
by the arch apoftate, to eat the prohib-
ited morfel, and awful was the confe-
quence. ∙ Having eat thereof herfelf,
fhe became her hufband's firft feducer,
and drew him contrary to the light of
his own confcience, to partake of her,
guilt. This done, the horrors of Ge-
henna tortured their guilty confciences,
and they knew not where to fly, to fhun
the —

the threatened death. The evening arrived, the sky had lost its serenity, the
beasts their wonted tameness, the flow-
ers loose the greatest part of their fragrance, and all nature seemed to wear
a melancholy aspect. On the evening
just as radiant Phœbus concealed himself in the western ocean, the Divine
Creator himself comes down into the
garden, to call the delinquents to account for their conduct. Awful was
the change. They cannot stand with
filial respect and confidence in the sacred
presence ; much less did they long for
the approach of the celestial visitant as
heretofore ; but basely fly from the sight
of their Maker, to hide themselves from
his researches ; whose amiable presence
erewhile, they counted the most exalted blessing. Nor did the eternal himself appear at this time with that friendly and familiar air as before, but with
resentment glowing on his awful countenance. The thicket unable to conceal the parents of mankind, from the
piercing eye of Omniscience, he ar-
raigns them at his equitable bar, hears
their

their poor defence, and denounceth. upon them the fatal fentence. Since then none may hope to touch forbidden fruit with impunity.. You my lady are like the interdicted tree. Your. amiable perfonal excellencies, difplay themfelves in the moft alluring manner.—— But they are forbid the enjoyment of all men, my lord alone excepted. He alone may approach you with familiarity. He alone may lawfully enjoy.—— Was I, Madam, to dare. injurioufly to betray my mafter,. and to difhonour his amiable confort,. I fhould act as a villain, and ungrateful traitor to.the beft of mafters, and as a rebel againft the God of my ancefters, whofe tremendous wrath I fhould thereby awake ; and you yourfelf, Madam, upon cool reflection would curfe me for perpetrating the execrable deed.. I love you miftrefs, and would protect, not difhonour you : I love my honourable lord, and would not betray him. I love my God, and would not offend him. Permit me then, Madam, to intreat you to ftifle a paffion fo deftructive to your hon—

our

our and tranquility ; which if indulged, will yield the moſt bitter reflections and expoſe to the greateſt dangers."

"Ah Joſeph ! replied the wife of Potiphar, what a well invented ſtory your icy heart has contrived, in order to evade the honours proffered you ? What needleſs ſcruples does that whim of religion and virtue inſpire you with ? What injury would thereby be done to your maſter, Joſeph ? I am ſtill his. Always ready to oblige him, and ſhould never behave to him with the greater diſtance. We have nothing to fear, ſo long as we are prudent enough to conceal our intercourſes from the curious eye. I tell you again, I love you Joſeph.

"Madam, returned the Hebrew, even in my father's family in the caſe of my only ſiſter, I have a loud monitor, that bids me beware of the ſin of uncleanneſs." "I pray now let us have it, ſaid ſhe, I ſuppoſe it is ſome whimſical religious ſtory, tending to the ſame purpoſe."

"It is a truth, Madam, the remembrance of which, will give occaſional ſorrow to me to my dying day. My ſiſter, young,

young, amiable, and curious, longing to
fee more of the world than her father's
houfe admitted of, went forth into a
neighbouring principality, at a time,
when a magnificent feftival, in honour
of their patron deity, was folemnized.
Amongft the multitude who attended,
were Shechem, the young prince of the
Hivites, and Tamar his fifter. Dinah,
young and vain, was attended with a
gaudy train felected out of my father's
menials, and fhe herfelf in an elegant
apparel. Prince Shechem caft a lan-
guifhing look upon my fifter, conceived
a violent paffion for her, and refolved
at all events to poffefs her. His fifter
Tamar, was young and beautiful, but
unadorned with that amiable virtue
which is the greateft glory of her fex.
She contracted an intimacy with my fifter Dinah, who unfkilled in amorous in-
trigues, accepted of an invitation to vifit the princefs Tamar, in the city of
Shechem. The day was fpent in innocent pleafantry, only every now and
then there was fomething that bordered
upon the profane. As the folar orb defcended.

fcended the weftern hemifphere, Dinah propofed her return to her father, but was put off from time to time, by the prince and princefs, till fhe was at laft convinced of her unhappinefs, and too late repented the curiofity that led her forth to fee the daughters of the land. She was not to be won by prayers and intreaties, therefore was forced to a compliance with his lewd defires, and for a time continued a prifoner to the prince's affection, within his palace. Still he loved her with encreafing fervour, and his very foul clave to the unhappy damfel. So courteous, affable, and loving was his conduct to her, after he had defiled her, that fhe half forgave the injury, and conceived fomething like affection for him. His love grew ftronger every day, and finding that he could not live without her company on the one hand, nor his affection permit him to ufe her like an harlot on the other, he implored the good offices of King Hamor his father, to procure her for him in lawful marriage. From motives of policy, the old king readily complied, propofed to

his

his courtiers the defire of his fon, and then made fuit unto Ifrael for his confent. My father called a council defcended from his loins, to deliberate on the propofal of Hamor ; and the iffue was, that unlefs the fubjects of that prince, would conform to the laws of the Hebrews, they would not confent, but would refcue their fifter by force of arms, or perifh in the attempt. This communicated to Hamor and Shechem, they made no difficulty of complying with the condition. A public feftival was appointed to be obferved by all ranks of the people to folemnize the marriage of Shechem and Dinah : on the firft day of which, every male was circumcifed in compliance with the Hebrews, and the carnival greatly inflaming the blood, and enervating their minds, they fell an eafy prey to the premeditated revenge of my brethren.— Simeon and Levi, Dinah's brethren, felected a choice band out of Ifrael's domeftic retinue, and clad in arms, before the dawn of the third morning of the feftival, came intrepidly upon the city,

and

and filled it with fearful carnage. King Hamor and his fon hearing the cry of murder from all quarters, alarmed the houfhold troops, but ere they could make refiftance, met with death in the gates of the palace royal. The city they reduced to afhes, and flew every man within it. This horrid flaughter and conflagration all arofe from the unlawfulnefs of Shechem's love. Had he obferved the rules of virtue, and propofed honourable terms to the Patriarch, he would no doubt have accepted of the alliance. But uncleannefs is not to be tolerated in the houfe of Ifrael. Now, my honorable lady, confider the difference between my lord Potiphar, firft of Pharaoh's martial train, and thefe fimple Hebrew fwains. If they could pour out defolation upon the metropolis of a kingdom, in revenge of their fifter's difhonor, what might not my lord do, was any villain to dare audacioufly to defile his honorable bed, and violate the chaftity of his betrothed lady? Far be it from Jofeph, Madam, to entertain a thought fo treacherous to either you or my lord."

I   She

She replied not, but disappointed in her love, continued the rest of the time full of silent discontent, her troubled mind agitated with different passions, gave place alternately to love, fear, and hateful revenge ; but the more that Joseph saw the agitations of her mind, the more steadily was his own heart fortified by virtue. Arrived at the palace, she retired to her chamber to consult with her nurse Syrena, what further should be done ; and afflicted Joseph went to his apartment to implore the protection of Jacob's God.

Syrena gave it as her opinion, that fear or modesty must needs be the cause of Joseph's refusal of an offer that did so much honour to a favourite menial ; alledging, that her mistresses graces, were sufficient to thaw the frigidity of even old age itself : and advised that a further trial should be made ere she gave up her hopes. Pharaoh's birthday was now at hand, and the general must repair to court, to compliment his majesty, and assist upon the grand occasion, but Sabrina was taken extremely

ly ill in the morning, with a palpitation of heart, and great depreffion of fpirits, and therefore could not attend him to the court. Her lord no fooner gone with his retinue, than fhe fends Syrena to command Jofeph to attend her pleafure in her chamber. Slow of pace, and with a reluctant heart, he came and ftood at a formal diftance from her, while in thoughtful filence fhe fat, her eyes intently fixed on his blufhing face. "And are you at laft come, faid fhe, ungrateful youth, to fcorn and flight your over fond miftrefs. Come nearer, Sir, and let me fpeak with freedom to you, for you and I muft be better acquainted before we part. It would have been better for you, and more becoming your character and ftation, to have complied at once, with my former requeft, if it had only been out of refpect to the dignity of my ftation, and the violent excefs of my paffion; and not have fuffered me to undergo the fhame of repeating my folicitations, and condefcending to exprefs myfelf in terms too ftrong for female modefty to

utter

utter without a blush.　But I am willing to put the moft favorable conftruction upon your conduct, and will **not** only make all poffible allowances for it, but endeavor to remove out of the way, every thing that would protract our pleafure.　Perhaps, Jofeph, you might entertain fome fufpicion, whether I was really in earneft at our laft interview, or if I did not make that humble proftration of myfelf to you, on purpofe to try your virtue.　But affure yourfelf that I was in earneft, as my repeating the fame requeft, might abundantly ferve to demonftrate.　But I'll tell you more Jofeph, and what would undo me, was it known to any but ourfelves.　This day I feigned myfelf fick, on purpofe to be at home with you.　The jolity of courtly parade, is nothing to your fweet company.　Now you may if you will, fee, that I can part with the company of nobles, and princes, for the love I bear to your amiable perfon, my Jofeph.——And fhall I languifh and pine without any hope of comfort, when it is in your power my dear friend to relieve me ? do

not

not talk any more to me of thofe holy ties of religion, thofe fevere rules of virtue. Virtue is a mere' imaginary thing, that can bring no pleafure, but only diftract the heart with terror. And what is religion, but a dream, as the lives of all our priefts teftify ; for however they cry out againft the fins · of the times, when in the pulpit, there are none that relifh gay delights better than they in private ? Could thy God, my Jofeph, delight in making thee behave cruelly to one that loves thee, he were to be detefted inftead of adored ; beware, Jofeph, and not father thy indifference to me upon the gods; rather own that fome happy unftained nymph has captivated your affections, and that for her fake you cannot, you dare not oblige your miftrefs. But cannot you be her's and mine too ? But oh ! your honor is concerned. Pray were is my honor in thus humbly fuing to you my friend ? but what is honour ? merely fantaftic and precarious. Honour is certainly to eafe · the pains of thofe that love us."

"Oh madam ! returned he, with a

figh fufficient to rend his loins, what avails a momentary pleafure that foon muft be devoured by keen remorfe? Once done it cannot be recalled, let the repentance be ever fo poignant. Concealed by thefe curtains, will not fecure us from the fears of difcovery and difgrace. I might indeed join with you to difhonour my lord, and for a moment we might riot in the pleafures of fenfe. But, alas! what would this be in comparifon of the folid pleafures of a good confcience? Equal if not fuperior delights are lawful to you in your marriage relation with him, to whom you gave yourfelf. And where can a man be found more amiable and more defirable for a bofom companion, than my lord? Think my lady how far what you propofe would debafe you below your rank, to come to a level with your poor fervant, whom you may at all times command in every thing lawful. No, Madam, I affure you, I cannot confent to a deed fo bafe, as wilfully to injure the benevolent Potiphar, difhonor the God of my fathers, and bring an indelible

ble ftain on the family of Ifrael. Far from being like idols of ftocks & ftones, my God fees our moft fecret actions ; he hears our fofteft whifpers, and tries the deepeft receffes of thought. Urge me not, Madam, for I cannot commit this great wickednefs in the fight of my God." He ended here, and fhe full of refentment replied.

" It might have been fufficient, mo-deftly to have refufed the offer which the excefs of my paffion urged me to make, without upbraiding me with my fhame. This argues impudence, joined with an unrelenting heart ; but I leave it for you to choofe, whether you will kindly embrace your own happinefs, and render happy her that loves you to dif-traction ; or to ftand the fhock of my revenge, for revenged I will be ; thefe charms for which princes have fighed in vain, are not to be flighted with impu-nity. No, Sir, never think of it. I fhall certainly accufe you to your mafter of having attempted my difhonour, and a dry oftentation of virtue, the moft folemn proteftations of innocence, will not then

deliver

deliver you from the fangs of punifhment.

O Jofeph! never was virtue affault-
ed like thine.   Never did youth more
glorioufly triumph over temptation.——
Neither prayers, tears, nor threatnings
upon her part, compaffion nor terror
upon thine, could alter the purpofes of
thy determined virtue, and make thee
yield to the importunity of a difhoneft
appetite.. Amiable youth, how fwelled
thy noble heart with generous pity for
thy betrayed mafter ; and with grief for
thy fallen miftrefs ? Even the danger
that on all hands furrounded thee, could
not ftem the chryftal tide, that ran
down thy manly cheeks——while Sabrina,
fat with her eyes fixed upon thee, eyes
fparkling both with love and revenge.

Miftaken woman, fhe interprets Jofeph's tears in her own favour, and bent
on completing her own fhame, fhe lays
hold on him, and threw herfelf on the
bed, faying, "Come Jofeph, let us enjoy the prefent moment, whilft kindnefs
gently flows through your yielding
heart."

" No

" No, Madam, replied the fteady youth, dungeons and gibbets, are no objects of my fear. Criminal converfe with a forbidden object ; injuring my mafter, and offending my God, are what I juftly fear, and I am in danger of them all, whilft I am in your company. But I abhor the deed, and fly from the place of temptation. So faying, he turned haftily about, freed himfelf from her embrace, and rufhed from the room. Her luft grown to a fury unbridled, fhe ftrove to pull him upon the bed, when difentangling the diamond, which buttoned his purple fcarf, he left it in her poffeffion and fo efcaped the fnare.

The noble youth departed, obftinate in virtue, fhe was miferably diftracted between the fting of her difappointed love, and the fear of being difcovered, but foon fhe refolved the ruin of him who had goodnefs enough, not to ruin her even at her own requeft. She cried aloud as if in imminent danger, and nurfe Syrena, who gueffed at the caufe, flew to her affiftance. She found

found her fitting upon a bed, Joseph's scarf lying by her, and deeply bathed in tears.. " O what shall I do Syrena ? cried she, the scornful Hebrew despiseth my paffion, and fled but juft now from me, with as much horror, as if I had been a cockatrice.. Go nurfe,. alarm the houfe, and have him feized ; for I will fwear an attempt of ravifhment a- gainft him. Befriend me now but this once, my dear Syrena,. and I am your friend forever." The houfhold alarm- ed, Jofeph is feized and kept in confine- ment till Potiphar's return, which was in the evening ;. he went directly to his fpoufe's chamber, to enquire after her health, where he found her in the utmoft diforder and confufion, with the rage of her difappointed luft.. Struck with af-- tonifhment, he kindly enquired the caufe of her diforder..

" Alas ! my lord, faid this daughter of deceit, we have nourifhed up a viper to fting us, a wretch that will undo us, if permitted under the roof. The in- folent Hebrew, forgetting his wretch- ednefs when you was pleafed to take
him

him under your protection; and the friendly entertainment we have given him since he lived with us. Not content with being the sole difpofer of all your poffeffions, afpireth even to your bed. I was laid down to take a little flumber at noon, when the fellow came audacioufly into my chamber, and explained his beaftly defign. I chid his impudent lewdnefs, and charged him to be gone that inftant, or I would inform you of his conduct; but inftead of departing the villain laid hold on me, and by force would have obtained his filthy purpofe, had I not alarmed the houfe with my cries. When he found me inflexible, and heard the cries of my diftrefs, he hafted away in fuch diforder that he left his fcarf behind him; a fure teftimony of his villainy. My lord, you have profeffed to love me. If you do, you will revenge the infult offered to my honour, by inflicting the moft examplary punifhment upon this infolent wretch. I fhall never be able to endure the fight of him again about the houfe."

Highly

Highly delighted with the virtue and probity of his lady, and aftonifhed at the effrontery of the Hebrew, he commanded Jofeph to be brought pinioned into his prefence, and with a countenance, ftern as the face of war, thus accofted him. " Wretch ! What pity is it that thy outfide, and undaunted air fhould bely fuch a bafe and diabolical heart. I blame myfelf, wretch, that I ever fheltered thee under my roof, and placed fuch a villain at the head of my affairs. But thy vile hypocrify would deceive thofe that are even but a few degrees 'better than thyfelf : well then might thy faintly fhew, gain upon my artlefs heart, a ftranger to treachery and black defign. Wouldft thou, viper, bite the hand that feeds thee, and poifon the bofom that nourifhed thee ? Was it not enough that I had put my all into thy untrufty hands, but thou muft afpire even to my bed ? A gloomy dungeon fhall fuperfede the purple bed to which thou afpireft ; and rattling chains fhall ferve inftead of the foft careffes of unlawful

love.

love. Away with the flave to his def-
tined dwelling, till I have time to me-
ditate fome unheard of punifhment for
his bafenefs." The fame virtue that
preferved the pious Hebrew, in the
time of temptation, from the guilty
deed, preferved him now from fearing
the threats of his mafter, wherefore
with a fteady and undaunted air, he replied,

" Dungeons and chains, my lord, I
can defy, nor can even the approach
of death at all difturb the peace of my
heart. But your difpleafure, my lord,
I cannot fuftain. The hatred of my
kind and generous mafter ; once my
avowed friend, is worfe than a thoufand
deaths. But remember it Potiphar,
Jofeph is clear from the guilt charged
againft him, and his own confcience
cannot accufe him of fo much as a difhoneft thought of this kind. I believe
in God. The God of my father in due
time, will bring me forth to the light,
and I fhall behold his righteoufnefs in
clearing up my innocence, and expofing to infamy the bafenefs of my accuf-

K   ers,

ers, of what rank foever they be." He-
faid, and inftantly was conducted to jail,
with a ftrict charge to the keeper, to
lade him with the heavieft irons, and to
fhut him up in the clofeft ward.

THE

THE

LIFE

OF

JOSEPH.

ARGUMENT.

Gabriel ascends to heaven to receive fresh
instructions—Rachel & Thirza the wife
of Shem, descend and comfort him un-
perceived—Potiphar called in a hurry
to fight the Ethiopians, forgets Joseph—
Their discourse—Chorion the jailor, has
a dream that impresseth his mind with
tenderness—The night following, sees an
heavenly apparition go to Joseph's apartment—Gabriel appears to Joseph, instructs and comforts him—The jailor's
reverence for Joseph—He gets acquainted
with the king's butler and baker—Their
dreams—The butler's interesting history
—The good interpretation of his dream
—The fatal interpretation of the baker's
dream—His former villainy and murder
—An apparition of his murdered brother
—The butler's restoration to his office—
Joseph falls in love with an unknown
princess—The baker's execution—Sabrina's passion for Joseph rekindles.

B O O K IV.

GABRIEL appointed guardian to the banifhed Jofeph, induftri-oufly ftrove to fortify his youthful mind againft the attacks of wickednefs. Seeing now the iffue, afcended fwifter by far, than the forked lightnings, to the regions of eternal day, to receive inftructions from the univerfal Governor, what to do in favour of his beloved charge. Mean while, Rachel, Jofeph's mother, and Thirza the wife of Shem, riding on a golden cloud, were taking a tour through this part of the univerfe ; and feeing the lovely youth conducted to prifon, they defcended low, and breathed ambrofial fragrance into the dungeon, a little to mitigate his forrow. "O Thirza, faid Jacob's departed fpoufe, how deep and intri-

cate

cate are the ways of the Almighty to us, whilft in a ftate of dark mortality? Who could from his prefent circum-ftances think, that in the divine pur-pofe, my Jofeph fhould be placed at the head of his brethren from whom he is feparated? Who could fuppofe that the lovely prifoner is to be the future protector of the chofen feed? The archers have indeed galled thee fore my fon, but thy bow has ftill abode. in its ftrength; by the mighty God of thy father Jacob, fhall the arms of thy hands be made ftrong, and thefe thine enemies, fhall yet bow down un-. to thee. O Jacob! thou dear, thou honourable man. What pangs would wring thy forrowful heart, didft thou. but know the agonies of thy beloved? But thou art foothed under the kind deception, believing his pain long fince to have been finifhed. His fuppofed death gave thee lefs forrow by far, than his prefent life would bring upon thee. Faith and patience, poffefs ye the heart of my darling, till he afcend triumphant over his enemies." "O

my

my Rachel ! my deareſt daughter, returned the wife of Shem, we have ever
ſeen, that whom the holy and allwiſe
God deſigns for eminent uſefulneſs, he
trains them up in the rough ſchool
of adverſity.. The afflictions my lovely deſcendant endures, will endue him
with ſympathy for the diſtreſſed : even
when aſcended to the government of
the kingdom, thy chains Joſeph, will
make thy grandeur to fit more graceful upon thee. The falſe accuſations
laid againſt thee, will teach thee the
neceſſity of caution and impartiality in
the adminiſtration of juſtice.. Perſe-
vere in virtue my ſon. Take kindly
the rough means by which thy heavenly father inſtructeth. The end ſhall
crown the work, and fill thy heart with
gratitude, and thy mouth with praiſe.''
Thus the two mothers converſed together, after the manner of diſembodi-
ed ſpirits, and gently moved forward
upon their cloudy chariot, leaving the
perfumes of life behind them.

Chorion the jailor, had juſt ſecured
his new priſoner in irons, made faſt
the

the prifon, and retired to reft, when he
fell into a deep fleep, from which he
was awaked by the following dream.—
He fuppofed himfelf in a widely ex-
tended field, ruminating on the beauties, which every where decorated the
teeming earth.   Walking flowly along,.
a yearling lamb, clofely purfued by a
couple of wolves, run up to him, and
fell down at his feet, as if fupplicating
protection.   Untimidated, the fhe wolf
came rufhing forward, and with bloody
fangs, was for devouring the innocent
even before his face, whilft he drew
his fabre to defend the fugitive.   In
the midft of the fcuffle betwixt him
and the ravenous monfter, he awoke
with an impreffion upon his mind, that
fome prifoner under his care was per-
fonated by the lamb, perfecuted by
enemies, who eagerly thirfted for his
blood, and hoped to find that fafety
and friendfhip in the cells of a prifon,
which were denied him where he had
a right to expect it.   Chorion was none
of the favage herd, who have in later
times kept watch at the doors of pri-

son-houses. He had a humane heart, capable of feeling the distresses of his fellow creatures. The necessary strictness and severity of his office, was always performed with a reluctant hand, and with inward sensations, becoming a descendant of Adam.

The dream was suggested at Gabriel's request, by one of the benevolent etherial spirits, with a view to render Chorion as gentle as might be to Joseph, during the absence of his guardian angel, who upon his account, was ascended to the empyrean. It had its desired effect, for the cautious jailor, for fear that he should add to the sufferings of the innocent, was extremely gentle and tender to all his prisoners.

The following night having spread the thickest darkness over all the land, neither moon nor star embellished the concave sky. As Chorion stood upon his tower, he saw at a distance, darting through the air, a form divinely beautiful and fair, surrounded with glory, almost too strong for his visual orbs to sustain.

fuftain, and followed by a train of ftu-
pendous fplendour, which evidently
befpoke the vifitant, to be of celeftial
lineage.   As he drew near, and went
paft the keeper to the prifon, he had
as good a view of him, as his confufion
would fuffer him to take.   For Jofeph's
fake, the friendly angel thought proper
to favour Chorion with a glimpfe of
etherial brilliance, and but a glimpfe,
left he fhould by too rich a difplay
of celeftial excellence, overturn the
reafoning powers of his mind.   Some
heavenly deity, cried Chorion in a
rapture, fome God who defends virtue
and innocence, propitious to. the cries
of diftrefs, condefcends to vifit the
loathfome cells of a miferable prifon.
See, he is gone directly to the ftranger's apartments.   The youth is innocent of whatever he is accufed of ;
the holy Gods will not condefcend to
vifit the guilty.   This is the lamb that
fled to me for protection.   O lovely
youth, as far as poor Chorion's influence can go, you fhall meet with nothing but friendfhip within thefe walls.

I .

I will eafe you of your chains, and provide fuitable apartments for your reception.

Mean while Gabriel ftood confeft in Jofeph's cell, and even groaned to fee the fon of Ifrael incumbered with horrid chains. Secretly he gave him a celeftial draught juft drawn from the fountain of life, which enabled him with pleafure to bear the heavenly radiance with which he was arrayed. "Fear not Jofeph, faid the fplendid meffenger, I am Gabriel of whom thou haft often heard. Gabriel who ftands in the prefence of the Lord. This is the firft time indeed of my appearance to thee, but thou haft long been my careful charge. It was I that fent Abel thy kinfman to comfort thee when thou waft in the pit. I ftood by with unfpeakable pleafure and beheld the noble refiftance you made to the temptations of your miftrefs : and rejoiced to fee you come off a conqueror from danger fo fatal. Your prefent afflictions my Jofeph are not the fruit of guilt on your part. They are fuch as you fhall
be

be delivered from. But, O, what keen remorfe would have torn your heart had you been left Jofeph to fin fo loudly againft your God ! From fome inkling which the infernal fpirits had got of the defigns of your God towards you, they have leagued together to deftroy you ; and two of the moft active of the damned race, as agents for the rebellious community, undertook to accomplifh your ruin. Belphegor and Adramelech, they ftirred up your brethren against you, and had not I interpofed, your blood would have been facrificed to their malice. Little did they know that the very means which they took to fruftrate the defigns of grace were appointed directly to promote them, and that whilft they were gratifying their own infernal malice, they were doing what fhould be over-ruled to your advantage. They inflamed your miftrefs with a burning defire to enjoy your embraces, and turned her love into hatred and rage upon being difappointed. And it was them who infpired Potiphar with the rafh defign of deftroying

ftroying you. Thus far they have been divinely permitted to perfecute you Jofeph. But here ends the bounds of their permiffion, Truft in the God of thy fathers. Let patience have its perfect work ; for when thou art tried, thou fhall come forth as purified gold.—— Grieve not for your father, for you fhall yet fee him in a ftrange land ; and thefe hands of yours fhall clofe his aged eyes, after you have received the paternal benediction from his prophetic lips.—— Potiphar will foon have his attention attracted by other objects, fo that he fhall not touch your life ; you will yet fee him and embrace him as your friend, for Sabrina fhall one day be made to confefs her guilt. I leave you Jofeph, but remember you the God of your fathers, and ferve him with a perfect heart. I have prejudiced the keeper much in your favour. The peace of the everlafting covenant be with you." So faying he fhrouded himfelf in darknefs and the young patriarch faw him no more. But O ! what pleafure did the feraph's melodious voice caufe to

L   thrill

thrill through the heart of the prifoner.
Even in a prifon he was wrapt up into
the fuburbs of heaven.   As foon as the
morning began to dawn, Chorion the
keeper from whofe eyes fleep had been
banifhed all the night, vifited every a-
partment in prifon, and when he came
fo Jofeph's cell he ftood motionlefs with
awful reverence of his prifoner ; and as
foon as he could fpeak, with a faultring
voice he faid, "I am forry, Sir, that
you have been fo ill ufed.   I wifh I had
known your defert before, then thefe
fervile chains fhould not have difgrac-
ed your limbs."   So faying he took off
his irons, led him up to his own apartments, and treated him with the utmoft refpect.

That very day a courier from the
frontiers of the kingdom arrived at the
war-office, with advice that the Ethiopians, then a warlike people, had invaded thofe parts of the empire moft con-
tiguous to them ; wherefore Potiphar
was difpatched at the head of the army
to put a ftop to their ravages ; an ex-
pedient that took off his attention from
Jofeph,

Joseph, and kept him long at a distance from Memphis. During which time, our injured hero continued a prisoner, neglected and forgot.. But the same divine & ever-watchful Providence which prospered him in the house of Potiphar, followed him still in the house of his prison, and succeeded all the works of his hands..

Amongst the many prisoners that were confined for different crimes were Florillo the king's principal cup-bearer, and Labonah the chief baker. Having received charge of all the prisoners from Chorion the keeper, Joseph frequently visited them, and soon contracted an intimacy with them. Making his morning visit to Florillo and Labonah, one day after he had been near a year in prison, he found a pensive sadness louring upon their heavy countenances.—— "What is the matter with you my friends said he ? It appears by your countenances that your hearts are sorrowful. May I beg to know the cause ? If any thing within my power can be of service to you, my assistance may be depended upon."

upon." "Alas, Sir! replied the butler, affiftance can come from the immortal Gods alone. Our cafe feems to be beyond the arm of humanity to remedy. Each of us have had a dream ominous of fome important event, but what it may portend is to us a fecret involved in the moft cloudy myftery."

Jofeph obferved that dreams are not always to be regarded, and even fuch as are fignificant and ominous muft have their interpretation from heaven. "Will you tell me your dreams, faid he, for fome I have interpreted? And I promife you at leaft I will not deceive you. But it would add greatly to the kindnefs, if you would give me with your dreams fome account of your paft lives, and I in my turn will freely communicate to you every material part of my own hiftory."

"I am, faid the butler, the only fon of Arba an Elamite, who dying when I was very young, left me under the care and direction of Athgar, my uncle by the mother's fide. The tender and delicate ufage which I experienced from

my

my parents, was changed into rough
and rigorous treatment by my uncle ;
and although fo very young, I was made
to feel the difference between paternal affection, and the guardianfhip of
the neareft kinfman.. Poffeffed of my
father's fubftance, which he was to hufband to my advantage, he relifhed the
fweets of it fo much, that he entertained thoughts of keeping it as his own
property, and took care to let me know
that I was folely dependant upon him
for the means of my fubfiftence. Con-
fcious that, in a land of oppreffion,
where my uncle had principal rule, there
was little profpect of power giving place
to equity ; I was obliged for my own
fafety patiently to bear my injuries ;
imagining, upon no ill ground, that
complaint of the grievances I fuffered
would only add to the weight of my
oppreffions. It was not long before
Cufhi, an enterprifing prince of a neighbouring people, upon fome flight pre-
tence quarrelled with the king of Elam
and invaded his territories. I was fent
to the war by my uncle's command, and

I

I had reafon to fear with a view to rid me out of the way. But you may think that I had but little heart to fight in defence of a land where I had fuffered fuch bafe oppreffion. Our army was far from being either fpirited or difciplined like the Hummims under Cufhi. The Elamites of diftinction wallowed in luxury, whilft thofe of inferior rank groaned under oppreffion. Therefore, when they came to face the enemy, they could make but a faint refiftance, and foon fought for fafety in rapid flight. Many were cut to pieces as they fled, and many were taken prifoners by the Hummims, amongft whom I was one. It was my lot to be brought to Memphis, and fold to one of the ftewards of Pharaoh's houfhold; and I muft fay in honour of my lord, that I have met with more hofpitable friendfhip, although a flave in the royal palace, than I ever received under my uncle's roof, where my own property fhould have procured me welcome.

"But the barbarous man did not
long

long enjoy either my eftate or his own, for the Elamites unable to ftand before the Hummims, Cufhi foon became mafter of the whole kingdom and divided it among his faithful followers. Meanwhile I was put into the loweft and moft fervile office in the palace; which was much more agreeable to me than to live near to a kinfman; who had in my perfon violated all the laws of hofpitality. My advancement was by flow degrees from one place to another, till it pleafed his majefty to enfranchife me, and place me near his perfon. I had long ferved in the capacity of cupbearer; when his majefty was taken with a violent diforder in the vifcera, which his phyficians judged to be the effect of poifon; and as I had the infpection of all the wine which he drank, and my friend Labonah of all the fruits and baked meats prefented at the royal table, we were by fpecial order feized and committed to prifon till further orders. But far be it from Florillo fo much as to wifh the leaft inconvenience to his royal mafter. May heaven preferve serve the life of Pharaoh to be a blessing to the land whatever becomes of me. Last night I had a dream which greatly disturbs me, apparently big with some important event.. I thought there was a vine before me, which divided itself into three luxuriant branches, each of which blossomed, budded, and bro't forth the most delightful grapes that I had ever beheld, and that in the greatest plenty. I tho't that I took of the grapes that were fully ripe and pressed them into Pharaoh's onyx cup, and presented to him the most mellow and best flavoured wine that I remembered ever to have seen. His majesty drank the wine, and smiling said, he hoped I would always procure him such wine as this, upon which I awoke full of anxiety about the event."

" My friend, said the son of Jacob, for your having drank of the cup of affliction, entitles you to that endearing appellation. You may make yourself very easy about your dream, for the God of heaven, who regards the cry of the oppressed, sends you by me a good
interpretation

interpretation of it. Before you was a luxuriant vine ; a gift of God to un-deferving men, the fruit of which compofeth differences, creates friendfhip, diffolves care and melancholy, and turns our fadnefs into joy. The three branches, are three days, which fhall be productive of great events in your favour, for on the third day, the king fhall raife you up out of the prifon, reftore you to your office, to the good graces of your mafter, and to the glowing embrace of your wife and children. I beg Florillo, that you may think of me. I have un-dergone oppreffions, at leaft equal to yours, and am here unjuftly confined, for preferring my own, and my mafter's honour, to the brutal pleafures of the flefh. It will be eafy for you, when you regain your mafter's confidence, to make mention of me to him, and pro-cure my releafe."

Labonah, the cook, having heard the favourable interpretation of his com-panion's dream, and hoping that his would be equally fo, began and related

it

it to Joſeph, as follows.   " I thought I
had upon my head, three baſkets made
of the whiteſt oſier, filled with proviſion
for Pharaoh's table ; in the firſt baſket
was bread, made of the kidney of the
fineſt wheat ; in the ſecond, were all
manner of taſteful viands ; and in the
third and uppermoſt were ſavory baked meats, ſuch as my maſter loveth.——
But in ſpite of all my care, as I paſſed
along, I could not preſerve my charge
from the rapine of the filthy birds, which
eat the baked meats out of the uppermoſt baſket." "I pity your circumſtan-
ces, my friend, ſaid Joſeph, and wiſh
it was in my power to give comfort to
you : But your fate, alas ! is determined. The baſkets are three days, yet
within three days, the king will order
you to be beheaded, after which your
body will be hanged on a gibbet, and
the birds of the air, will eat the fleſh
from off your bones, nor will it be in
your power to ſhun the threatning evil.
What you have done to deſerve it, I
know not, but ſuch is the decree of un-
erring Providence. Let me therefore
                         adviſe

advise you, to make confeffion to the God of heaven, implore his mercy to pardon your fins, and grace to fit you for another world, for you have little more than two days to live in this. Let your cafe be ever fo defperate, with him there is mercy, and plenteous redemption to them who call upon him."

"I fee then returned Labonah, that judgment and juftice fleepeth not, but fometimes overtakes the offender, when he thinks himfelf moft fecure. I am indeed clear from every bad defign upon Pharaoh. A thought of poifoning him, never entered my mind. Yet I exafperated him, when I found myfelf arrefted without a caufe, and wifhed the deed to have been done, of which I was accufed, that I might have had fomething worthy of imprifonment and death. But this was only the effect of ungovernable paffion ; though according to the law of Egypt, it will be deemed high treafon, and worthy of death. But alas ! although I count myfelf in this to be innocent, it is long fince I merited the death now to be inflicted

on

on me. So that however inequitable I account the fentence of Pharaoh, that of the Gods is juft. I am a Lybian by birth, Obed my father, left my elder brother and I, poffeffed of his whole eftate, which was very confiderable.— Ofmyn, my brother, was induftrious and frugal, by which means he greatly increafed his wealth, gained the friend-fhip of his fuperiors, and the veneration of people of lower birth. For my own part I minded nothing but pleafure, and thofe were my choiceft companions, who were the greateft voluptuaries. By thefe means my wealth was impaired, and I brought to wifh my niggardly brother, (as I then called him,) out of the way, that I might poffefs myfelf of his eftate. Glad would I have been if fome fatal accident had clipped the thread of his life afunder, but it was long before I could come to a refolution to deftroy him myfelf. However, at laft, by the advice of a lewd woman, I gave him a poifon that ftole infenfibly into the mafs of blood, and by flow degrees ftopped up the fprings of life. It was long before

fore its effect became apparent, though at laft it put a period to his days, and I took poffeffion of his eftate, as being his heir at law. Some years I lived in the quiet enjoyment of the fruits of my brother's toil and my own unrighteouf- nefs, when an unhappy circumftance o- bliged me to leave all behind, and feek for fafety in a foreign country.

Having contracted an intimacy with the wife of a confiderable man in the neighbourhood, I had the misfor- tune to ftay later than ufual one even- ing when the hufband was not expect- ed to come home, but to our utter con- fufion he entered the chamber and found us converfing criminally together. How nearly alas ! is one evil allied to another ? To conceal our fhame, and prevent him from obtaining legal re- drefs, I rofe in a fury, flew to my poig- nard, and plunged it into his breaft before he had time to reflect on his own difhonour. As I had perpetrated the horrid deed, I hafted from the fcene of murder, and retired to reft in my own apartment. In the third watch of the

M   night,

night, I was furprifed by a fuperna-
tural light, which darted into my chamber, and illuminated every corner of it.
Unufed to fuch phœnomena, my blood,
frcze in my veins, my hair ftood upright
on my head, and all the horrors of my
guilt ftared me in the face.   The light
increafed, and I clearly faw my brother
Ofmyn clad in celeftial attire, ftanding
by my bed fide, whilft he thus addreft
me.   " Wretched Labonah, will thy
murdering hand never be tired with
fhedding innocent blood ? Was it not
enough to poffefs yourfelf of my eftate,
by murdering me ; but you muft go
and violate your neighbour's bed ? And
was it not enough that you robbed him
of his honour, and his wife of her virtue, but like a villain, innured to bloodfhed, you muft drench your thirfty
fword in his honourable blood ? Do not
you fear the awful God, who hates injuftice and violence, and with whom no
unrepenting murderer can dwell ? can
you fpare no time from your riot and
wantonnefs to think but a little of the
tremendous audit, to which you will
                                        foon

foon be called ? Can you bear an eternity of unfpeakable torment, rather than forego your fenfual gratifications ? It is an awful choice, Labonah, yet that choice feems to · be yours. Arife guilty man, arife, and flee to fome foreign country, where the vengeance of man, will not be able to reach thee. But remember, the vengeance of God will follow thee even there, and bring thee to condign punifhment, both in this life and that which is to come, unlefs thou repenteft of, and forfakeft thy vicious habits." So faying the vifion departed, and as foon as fomewhat recovered from my fright, I collected all my money and jewels, and inftantly departed for Egypt ; in which kingdom I went through many fcenes too tedious to mention, before I rofe to the dignity of my late ftation. Too late I now fee, that honour and integrity, fhall preferve thofe who are guided thereby, and that however pleafant, fenfual indulgencies for the prefent may be, the end of them is bitter as wormwood."

Early on the third morning a chariot

ot rolled up to the gates of the prifon, in which was a reverend old man, whofe filver hairs hanged down in graceful ringlets upon his fhoulders ; he was come as Florillo's friend, with fpecial order to reftore the cup-bearer to his dignity. Along with this fenior prince, Jofeph beheld a young lady, who gave him much uneafinefs afterwards. She was that beauteous virgin Afenath, the only daughter of the prince of On, who was alfo high-prieft of Heliopolis. An artlefs modefty greatly improved the native elegance and matchlefs graces of her outward form. Her cheeks were a lovely mixture of the rofe and lilly, and her eyes a fprightly blue. Her hair in carelefs elegance defcended low, and partly covered the ftrings of jet and pearl, which adorned her comely neck. —The firft fight of her wounded the youthful fon of Jacob, and kindled an uneafy unknown paffion in his heart ; till now, he never had felt the vacuum left in his breaft for his other felf. But now the damfel had fixed her empire in his heart, and the lovely image of the fair

unknown

unknown wantoned perpetually before his eyes, whilft he languished for the abfent fubftance. But hopelefs was his paffion, he is a' prifoner, accufed of a capital tranfgreffion of the laws, and fhe a perfon of elevated rank. This, this, he cried, muft confound all my hopes, and I alas ! muft languifh under a wound incurable.

Florillo replaced in his office, a guard arrived at the king's command, and conducted defpairing Labonah to the place of execution, where Jofeph's prediction was amply verified upon him. But the courtier advanced again to favour, forgot the friendfhip of Jofeph the prifoner.

Sabrina's rage had long fubfided : her deadly hate, returned into female tendernefs, and kind relentings. Her thoughts repentant, accufe her rafhnefs. And O ! her heart is pierced with poignant pain at the thought, that her mad revenge caufes him, for whom fhe languifheth, to lay in an offenfive dungeon, whilft fhe had it not in her power, without expofing her own fhame, to admin-

ifter

ifter the leaſt conſolation to the injured
victim of her rage ; or procure the ſmall-
eſt degree of relief for herſelf.   And
thus ſhe languiſhed away a miſerable dying life at home, whilſt Potiphar was
dealing ſlaughter and death among the
warlike Ethiopians, and Joſeph lay neglected, and forgot in priſon.

" *A deep remorſe, from conſcience of her ſin,*
" *With conſtant horrors, vex her ſoul within ;*
" *Her thoughts ten thouſand racking torments feel,*
" *Yet in her treach'rous crime obdurate ſtill ;*
" *Her life and youthful ſpirits, melt away,*
" *Her beauty withers with a ſwift decay :*
" *By day ſhe wildly raves, conſumes the night,*
" *In thoughtleſs watchings, and imagin'd fright,*
" *While airy terrors glide before her ſight :*
" *Pale ghoſts with wide diſtracted eye-balls ſtare,*
" *And burning ſpectres, through the darkneſs glare."*

ROW.

THE

THE

L I F E

O F

JOSEPH.

ARGUMENT.

Pharaoh's two prophetic dreams—The convocation of
the clergy—The butler confesseth his neglect of Joseph
—Informs the king of his sagacity—He is brought
into the presence—He interpreteth the dreams—Pharaoh remembers to have seen him in his sleep, as re-
commended to him, as an assistant in government—
He is clothed in rich apparel—Potiphar comes to so-
licit Joseph's enlargement, Sabrina having confessed
the truth to him—He is astonished to find Joseph advanced so near the king—Joseph made lord-chancellor
of Egypt—builds granaries for receiving corn—
The king proposeth a marriage to him—He is greatly
perplexed, being already in love with an unknown lady—The match is proposed to the princess Asenath,
who rejects it ; having been in love with the Hebrew,
who rescued Sabrina from the lion, and not knowing
that lord-chancellor was he—Their astonishment and
joy at meeting, when Joseph finds Asenath to be the
lady whom he had loved with such vehemence, and
Asenath found her lovely Hebrew, to be the very person designed for her—The death of Judah's sons —
It renews his sorrow for his violence to Joseph.

B O O K V.

THE time of Jofeph's fufferings
elapfed : on the very night before
his enlargement the monarch had two
heaven-infpired dreams which baffled
the fkill of all his diviners. He fancied himfelf by the fide of the river Nile,
where the monfters of the flood fport
themfelves on the oozy fhore ; he faw
feven oxen of an enormous fize, fat and
well-fed, afcend out of the river ; and
feed upon the herbage of the neighbor-
ing verdant meadow : afterwards arofe
feven meagre and ill looking beafts,
upon which there feemed hardly to be
flefh enough to keep their bones together ; they alfo went and grazed on
the fame meadow, and prefently devoured all its verdure. Still hungry,
they fet upon' the fat oxen and eat up
them.

them likewife, and yet continued lean
and hungry as ever. A fight fo ftrange
in itfelf, impreffed the monarch's mind
fo deeply that he awoke in confufion,
and fleep departed from his eyes. Towards morning he dreamed again, and,
lo ! he was in the midft of a fertile field,
admiring the gifts of Ceres, when to his
wonder and furprife, there fprang up
inftantaneoufly feven of the largeft and
lovelieft ears of wheat that ever the
earth produced, and prefently after there
fprang up befide them feven thin and
blafted ears, which contained nothing
at all but duft and chaff ; and what was
very ftrange, the thin and blafted ears
fell upon and devoured the others, yet
ftill continued thin and blafted themfelves as before. Such were the dreams
of Pharaoh, and the interpretation was
given him likewife in his fleep, but a-
waking in confufion of mind the interpretation was gone and he retained only the dreams. Early in the morning
he fummoned a convocation of all fuch
doctors in the metropolis, that were
famous for learning in the Egyptian
                                    fciences.

fciences. Each appeared in the habit
of his order, trailing behind him the
enfigns of his reverence. But all in
vain their prieftly parade ; for the dumb
idols which they adored could not fpeak
the interpretation of the myftery. Every prieft has recourfe to different fchemes
of augury, and each produced different
interpretations from his neighbours,
but all of them rejected by the king,
who well enough knew that none of
them agreed with the interpretation
that he had feen in his fleep, although
he could not remember it himfelf. All
the attempts of the priefts became a-
bortive, and Pharaoh's rage kindling
againft them for their impofitions ; the
cup-bearer recollected his error, haften-
ed before the king, and thus humbly
addreffed him :

" O King live forever ! I humbly fue for pardon, as I have greatly
offended, and have not till now recollected my fault. Your Majefty may
well remember that falling under your
royal difpleafure the chief baker and I
were imprifoned. It came to pafs that
each

each of us had a dream on the fame night which greatly troubled us, as no interpretation could be found. I dreamed that before me was a noble vine bearing three luxuriant branches, each of which budded, bloffomed, and brought forth large clufters of grapes which ripened whilft I looked on, I held my lord's onyx cup in my hand ; took the grapes and preffed them into it and gave it into the hand of my lord to drink, your majefty drank and was highly pleafed with the flavour of the wine. The baker alfo dreamed, and lo ! upon his head were three bafkets, in the uppermoft of which was all manner of baked meat for Pharaoh, and as he brought them to the royal table, the birds of heaven defcended and eat the meats out of the bafket, nor could he keep them away. The next morning as we fat fad and forrowful, an amiable young man, an Hebrew, in whom is the fpirit of the holy Gods, and whom is there unjuftly confined, came in and interpreted both our dreams according to the event. The happy Florillo

rillo he reftored to his mafter's favour ;
but the wretched Labonah he hanged.
Will it pleafe my lord the king to order
the young man before you, and I doubt
not but he will interpret both of your
majefty's dreams."

The impatient monarch immediately ordered Jofeph to be brought from
prifon into the royal prefence. Cloath-
ed in decent apparel he came ready
prepared to give the king an anfwer ;
for Gabriel his friendly guardian had
appeared to him, and related both the
dreams and interpretation of them, and
withal gave him fuitable inftructions
relative to the government of Egypt.—
As he approached the throne with reverence, the eyes of all were attracted
by the graces of his perfon, which were
greatly enlivened by the blufh of modefty, which glowed upon his countenance. He bowed before the monarch,
and filently waited his commands.

The moment that Pharaoh beheld
the face of Jofeph, he faw fomething
in his countenance that attracted his
friendfhip ; he took him gently by the
hand

hand and faid, " There is a fervant of mine, who has given you the character of a very wife man, efpecially in the matter of opening hidden myfteries, of which he fays, he has had abundant proof in his own experience. I alfo had my dreams, the interpretation of which is dark and difficult, yet portending fome great event." Here he related his dreams, and required that Jofeph would lay afide all fear, and reveal the fimple truth, however difagreeable it might feem.

With a calm and ferene countenance, yet with an elevated air, that difplayed the majeftic dignity of his perfon, he replied. " Let Pharaoh give glory to the God of heaven, who in his great condefcenfion, makes known unto the king what he is about to bring to pafs on the earth : The dreams, my lord, were two in form, yet one in fubftance and fignification. The firft feven oxen and ears of corn, both mean the fame thing, and reveal to Pharaoh, that there fhall be feven years of fuch exceffive plenty of all forts of grain, as

was

was never known in any kingdom from the beginning ; as appears by the bulk and fatnefs of the firft feven oxen, and the largenefs and fulnefs of the firft feven ears of corn. The fecond feven meagre and ill-looking cattle, and the feven thin and blafted ears, denote alfo feven years of fuch fcarcity, as has never been known in the world, for there fhall be neither earing nor harveft ; and whereas the latter lean and ill-looking cattle, eat up the fat, and well favoured, and the thin and blafted ears, devoured thofe that were ripe and full ; it fhows that the feven years of plenty, will not produce fuffi-cient to fupply the feven years of fa-mine, unlefs the beft œconomy is eftab-lifhed in the land. Let my Lord the king confider, that the great governor of all, raifeth up certain men, to fover-eign rule over their fellow creatures, that they may be as fathers unto them, and provide for their peace, fafety and fupply. Thy God, O Pharaoh, who eftablifhed thy throne, hath not reveal-ed this to thee, with a view to afflict thy

royal

royal mind, but that by taking proper meafures for preferving the luxuriant fuperfluity of the firft feven years, thou mayeft be able to fupply the wants of thy people, during the feven years of famine, that they perifh not with hunger. Wherefore my advice is, that your majefty look out for fome wife and honeft man, fuitably qualified, and give him a commiffion for this purpofe, that the burden may be lighter upon the king."

The king looked with admiration at Jofeph, all the while he was fpeaking, aftonifhed to find fo much wifdom in a youth, and as foon as he had done fpeaking, fprung from the throne, and grafped him in his arms, with all the ardour of friendfhip, and faid, "Yes, this is the interpretation, and thou art the man, who was prefented to me in my fleep, to be my affiftant in a work fo great; I embrace thee therefore, as one fent by the God of heaven, to be a faviour to the people. And where, my lords, faid he to his courtiers, fhall we find one endued with wifdom and difcretion equal to him." Now the butler, who all this time ftood by, a filent but delighted auditor, came up, and tenderly embraced his quondam friend, begged pardon for his long neglect, and hoped that Joseph would not impute it to want of regard. Joseph told him, that the Lord's time was not till now come.

The king then gave command to the mafter of his wardrobe, to take Joseph away and clothe him in fuperb array. —Juft as he departed from the king's prefence one of the lords in waiting entered, and informed his majefty, that Potiphar, his general, waited in the hall, and requefted a private audience upon matters of great importance. Let him come in, faid the king, for he is a good man. The king retired with Potiphar, into an anti-chamber, and thus he preferred his fuit. " May it pleafe your majefty, immediately before I went by your commiffion againft the Ethiopians, I committed the fteward of my houfe to prifon, on my wife's accufing him with an attempt to ravifh her; it was

indeed

indeed my intent, to have fpoke to your
majefty, to have had him put to death ;
but thanks to the Gods, the fuddennefs
of the invafion, and the urgency of the
king's command, together with my regard for the public good, made me ut-,
terly forget my own affairs. My wife
upon my return hath withdrawn her
charge, intreating me to procure his
releafe, and indemnify him for his un-
juft imprifonment. This favour therefore, I would humbly intreat of your
majefty, and if it is agreeable, to take
him under your facred protection, for
he is one of the moft virtuous and wife
of the human race. Glad fhould I be
to enjoy him as my friend and companion in my own houfe ; but circumftances forbid his re-admiffion there."

The king heard with attention, and
rightly fufpecting that Jofeph was the
perfon in queftion, ordered him to be
brought again into his prefence. But
how great was Potiphar's furprife, to fee
his friend, his ill-ufed Jofeph, brought
unto the king clothed in purple, with a
chain of gold and diamonds about his
neck,

neck. He ftood motionlefs for fome time, then with an agitated voice, he abruptly faid, " It is he." And flying, to his embrace, he held him as if he grew unto him. Jofeph equally afton- ifhed on his part, to find fuch a change, faid, " I rejoice, my mafter, once more to embrace you as my friend ; and indeed, Sir, I never gave you caufe to be otherwife." " I know it Jofeph, I know it, returned he, but if his majef- ty will permit me, I will give you an account how it is that my friendfhip hath returned to its proper channel.

" You told me Jofeph, on that de- tefted night that I fent you to the dun- geon, that the God whom you and your fathers adore, would by fome means or other clear up your inno- cence, and detect the guilt of your accufers. It is done my friend, your prediction is fulfilled. Your poor un- happy miftrefs has paid dearly for her folly ; fhe is a proper object of your pity, let her then be ever free from your refentment. The accurfed nurfe, the wretched Syrena, was more to blame

than

than my fond Sabrina.   But I was
more to blame than both.   How could
I think that female virtue, could be
infenfible of your attracting charms ?
I delighted-to prefent you to her, rejoiced to fee her at any time look
friendly upon you, not confidering the
danger to which I expofed my poor
unhappy wife.. Whereas I ought to
have concealed you entirely from her
fight.. But I expofed her to the fnare,
and I wonder not if fhe was entangled.
I grieved to fee her beauty fade away
like the decaying rofe, and all her
wonted vivacity changed into a fettled
melancholy.   She loft all tafte for
pleafure, for amufements, company, or
drefs ; her fleep was unfeafonable, and
difturbed with diftreffed dreams. And
oft have I heard her in fecret, mourning
her betrayed lord Potiphar.. Cautious
of adding to her diftrefs, I avoided
fearching into the caufe of it. Till
laft night, fhe fent for me into her
apartment, where fhe has been for feveral days confined to her bed danger-
oufly ill of a fever. " O my lord !
                                   faid

said she, can you forgive the most
wretched creature, that ever was confided in by an indulgent and over cre-
dulous husband ? I have betrayed you
my lord, and I cannot die without in-
forming you of my guiltiness. Had
the injured Hebrew been no more
virtuous than Sabrina, your bed had
been stained with the vilest pollution."
What, cried I, is he not guilty ? " No,
my lord, returned she, he is not guilty,
his virtue is inflexible. Neither tears,
intreaties, nor threats could shake his
steady mind. He trusted in his God,
and was delivered. I alone am guilty.
—I conceived an involuntary passion
for him, the first time you presented
him to me. Conscious of its baseness,
I did what I could to stifle it ; but do
what I would, it grew stronger upon
me, till it burned as a flame intolerable.
Encouraged by my nurse, I gave scope
to my wild desires, did all that I could
to entice him, but to no purpose. His
regard to his God, and his master, prevailed over all my charms and snares ;
and by his stability he hath convinced
me,

me, that there is fomething in piety and
virtue, which I am unacquainted with.
O my lord ! may I hope to hear the
voice of your forgivenefs before I depart. And O ! how heartily could I
beg forgivenefs of injured virtue, was I
not fearful that the fight of the Hebrew
would overcome me."

" Yes Sabrina, replied I, I forgive
you with all my heart ; this honeft, this
frank confeffion, is a certain fign of
returning virtue. I embrace you my
love, and will haften Jofeph's enlarge--
ment, and reinftate him in the family.
" Oh ! never, never, anfwered fhe ; I
fhall not dare to behold him again ; for
although I feel nothing but the moft
laudable friendfhip for him now, I fhall
never dare to expofe my weaknefs to
danger fo imminent any more. Do you
my lord, what you can to ferve him in
any other way, but do not let me fee
him. When I am dead you may ufe
your difcretion, but fave your poor, weak
and unftable fpoufe from temptation !
She faid, and I promifing to comply
with her requeft, left her to reft. Hav-

ing

ing unburdened her mind, she slept compofedly all the night, and I have not feen fuch calm ferenity on her countenance for a long time, as this morning when I vifited her, before I came to wait on his majefty.

" But I fee Jofeph that your God in whom you trufted, would not permit Potiphar to have the pleafure of prefenting you to the king; but whofoever he is, that has that honour, shall be my friend forever." Pharaoh replied, " Jofeph hath prefered himfelf to my regard, and your ftory Potiphar hath riveted him in my efteem. It ferves to illuftrate and confirm what the native lovelinefs of his features indicate; and let me fay, it does not a little embellish the character of my noble captain, to be fo ready to repair an injury done through mifinformation.—Go home, my good lord, and let poor, penitent Sabrina know, that Jofeph is fecond in dignity and power in the kingdom of Egypt. The particulars of which, you shall be informed of Potiphar, at another time."

The

The fame virtue that enabled Jofeph to bear with fortitude the adverfi-
ty to which his innocence had expofed
him, enabled him now to hear his
praife echoed from one to another,
without pride or vanity. His purple
robe, and almoft imperial dignity, al-
tered not the native humility and modefty of his mind whereby he retained
his dignity unenvied by thofe of inferior
rank.

Pharaoh iffued a royal proclamation,
in which he nominated Jofeph as high
fteward of Egypt, and required all his
fubjects, of what rank foever, to be aid-
ing and affifting to him, in whatfoever
work he fhould undertake, or in what-
foevor elfe he might require. Jofeph,
on his part behaved with fo much equity, difcretion, and benevolence, that
the people in general rejoiced to fee the
reins of government put into a hand fo
fuitable.

Advanced to power, the firft thing
he did was to eftablifh the ftricteft
œconomy at court, to abridge the
king's expences, as much as confifted
with

with the dignity of fo great a monarch, that the exchequer might furnifh him money fufficient to buy up all the overplus of annual grain, and provide proper repofitories for receiving it, when purchafed. A fquare mile, on a pleafant meadow adjoining to Memphis, was felected for the feat of his granaries. The fpring approached, and every thing in nature appeared to bear a fertile appearance, for the earth brought forth not in its ufual courfe, but in great abundance. At the clofe of the year Jofeph iffued a proclamation, wherein he fignified by royal authority, that at the king's granaries a certain price would be given for all the corn that fhould be delivered to the fervants in waiting. The proclamation brought prodigious quantities of corn from all parts of the kingdom, as foon as the overflowing of the Nile enabled them to bring it by water carriage; and this was continued annually for the fpace of feven years, by which time he had filled every place that he could procure with grain.

O   One

One day king Pharaoh took him into his clofet, and thus addreffed him, " Jofeph, I and Egypt in general have reafon to confider you as a preferver and redeemer, raifed up unto us againft the day of calamity. As your God has been pleafed to fend you amongft us, it behoves us to do what we can to make your accommodation agreeable. I have propofed a match for you Jofeph. Nay, do not be furprifed : it is with one of the firft ladies of the Egyptian empire for birth, beauty and virtue. I intend to befpeak her for you this very day. Had I a daughter of my own, that I deemed worthy of you, fhe fhould be your bride ; but as I cannot thus gratify myfelf, I have fought out one to whom I think, even the greateft of monarchs can have no objection." " I beg, faid Jofeph, that you majefty will leifurely think of it, before you propofe a matter of fuch importance. How would a princefs of Egypt be debafed in being given to a mean, and once unhappy foreigner, whofe birth comparitively is obfcure ?"

" Say

" Say no more of it replied the king, for the matter is already determined. It will be an honour to the greatest princess to be advanced to your bed."

This advantageous offer, met not with that agreeable reception with Joseph, as one would have expected. The fair unknown whom he had seen whilst a prisoner, had captivated his heart : for her he languished in secret, and could admit of no thoughts of another to have place in his mind. He knew not well how to conduct himself in a matter so delicate, but at all events he resolved to do no injustice to his first love, although unknown, by admitting a second to his embrace.— Prince Potipherah being then at court, king Pharaoh proposed to him a match between Joseph, lord high-chancellor of the kingdom, and the lovely Asenath, his virtuous daughter. The proposal was heartily embraced by the reverend prince, and at his master's command he went home to consult his daughter's inclinations. But how great was his surprise to find Asenath utterly

averse

averſe to the honourable compact. "I entreat my father, ſhe cried, with tears like pearls dropping down her cheeks; I entreat that you will not oblige me to marry a man for whom I have not the ſlighteſt degree of deſire, and who ſince this propoſal, is become the object of my real averſion." "What objection can you have Aſenath, replied he, to the lord high-chancellor, the favourite of both king and people? Inconſiderate woman, it is the greateſt honour the king can confer upon you; and I inſiſt on your embracing it, otherwiſe give me a plain account of your reaſons for refuſing it." "Ah, Sir! ſaid ſhe, the lord high-chancellor is not the man who can make me happy, and I would not marry till I can have the proſpect of being happy in my huſband."

Young Aſenath was one of the party, who to grace the nuptials of Potiphar and Sabrina, went to hunt the monſters of the deſart, and had ſeen the young Hebrew's diſtinguiſhed gallantry, in reſcuing his miſtreſs from the
ferocity

ferocity of the desperate lion. Her young and tender heart, could not but feel the impreffion of the many graces of his amiable perfon ! but his generous valour moft fenfibly touched her. In fhort, fhe conceived a moft ardent and virtuous paffion for him, and refolved that if ever fhe fhould enter into the marriage relation, Jofeph, the gallant Hebrew, fhould be the man of her choice. But feeing nothing of him for a long time, fhe conceived a diflike to all other men : and notwithftanding the fame of the lord high-chancellor refounded through every Egyptian manfion, fhe never had the curiofity fo much as to look upon him.

It was infifted on however, by Pharaoh and Potipherah, that fhe fhou'd have an interview with Jofeph ; notwithftanding, they had both of them too much goodnefs, abfolutely to force the inclinations of either. But when they met, what a delightful furprife was it to Jofeph, to realize in Afenath the features, the air, and the very perfon of the lovely virgin, whom he had feen

Q 2   whilft

whilft a prifoner ; and for whom, altho'
unknown, he had renounced the whole
female race ? Nor was Afenath's furprife
inferior in viewing in the perfon of lord
high-chancellor, every feature and gef-
ture of her almoft adored Hebrew. Never did two come together with more
confummate averfion to each other, and
never were two more agreeably difappointed. "And is it you my lovely fair,
for whom I fo long have fighed, that
unknown to me his majefty defigned
for my fpoufe ? faid Jofeph, O my love,
you cannot conceive what antipathy I
entertained againft you ; but bleffed
be the God of heaven, who brings the
object of my warmeft wifhes to my
bofom." "And can it be poffible,
that you my lord are the very deliverer
of the fair Sabrina, faid Afenath ? Ever
fince that jovial day, the noble, the
gallant Hebrew, has been the fole lord
of all my affections. What a bleffed
Providence is this, that crowns my
wifhes by contradicting my inclination ;
for I hated you, Jofeph, I hated the lord
high-chancellor of Egypt, for the fake

of

of my amiable Hebrew. Let us adore the wifdom and goodnefs of that God, who has in fuch a defirable manner dif-appointed our fears." The nuptials were folemnized the enfuing day, in the prefence of the monarch. Great joy abounded amongft the people upon the occafion, and every body wifh-ed profperity to the new married cou-ple.

Whilft Jofeph continued profper-oufly to govern Egypt, it pleafed God to vifit eloquent Judah with a remem-brance of his former treachery. Er, his firft born, mature in years, married a damfel whofe name was Tamar, young, beautiful, and virtuous; in many refpects furpaffing her fellows. Er, was atheiftical and profligate, dif-regarded the commands of Abraham's God; and fought only to gratify a fen-fual appetite, and wallow in the plea-fures of the flefh. Judah and Shuah his parents, endeavoured to correct the irregularties of his life, by wholefome precepts and examples; but all their inftructions he foolifhly rejected, and

fought

fought for death in the error of his way. His difposition was the very reverfe of Jofeph's amiable qualities ; virtue was the delight of the one, but vice alone was the purfuit of the other. It happened on a day, that Er was fent to a diftant part of the country upon fome rural bufinefs, when going paft a fatal thicket, a panther fprung from the midft of it, and inftantly tore him to pieces. Not returning at the time expected, meffengers were difpatched to feek for him, and found him miferably torn by that monfter of the wood.——Then it was that Judah began to realize in his own experience, the heart wringing agonies of his father upon Jofeph's bloody coat being prefented to him. Then the pathetic addrefs of his fuppliant brother, begging for life, returned to his mind, with all its affecting circumftances. And to the lofs of his fon, he had the painful reflection of its being a juft judgment of the Omnipotent upon him, for having joined his brethren to bring affliction upon chofen Jacob.

That.

That the name of the elder born might not become extinct in Judah's family, Tamar was given to Onan, that feed might be raised up to his deceased brother. But Onan's heart being attracted by other charms, and knowing that fhould the marriage bed become fruitful, the children would not bear his name ; he took care to prevent the fruits of their intercourfe, though he did not altogether deny the pleafures of the conjugal ftate. What he did, was offenfive to the eye of infinite holinefs, and the Moft High to avenge himfelf of his impiety, ftruck him dead with a blaft of lightning darted from the æreal ftores of wrath.

O Judah ! how fenfibly was thy heart affected by this fecond ftroke of the divine hand ? How didft thou read thy fin in thy punifhment ! Both thy fons fnatched away by death, in the prime of their days. Tamar, thy daughter-in-law, had the bitternefs of burying two hufbands, ere fhe reached the meridian of life. Shelah alone, young and tender, fupport the hopes
of

of thy family. How did thy heart pant with jealous fear, left vengeance fhould write thee down childlefs, and fummon young Shelah to follow his elder brethren. Nothing but the fear of Simeon and Levi, kept Judah back from making a full confeffion of his guilt before the venerable patriarch. But the fear of them reftrained him ftill from duty, efpecially as he could never hear in what manner the Ifhmaelites had difpofed of Jofeph,

THE

THE

L I F E

OF

JOSEPH.

ARGUMENT.

Joseph purchaseth all the spare corn in E-
gypt, for seven years—The famine begins
to be felt—Jacob sendeth his sons down
to Egypt to buy corn—Simeon's dream by
the way—They are brought before Joseph
—He knows them, but they know not him
—He questions them strictly, and chargeth
them with being spies—They study to clear
themselves of the charge—He proposeth to
send one of them to bring Benjamin down—
That is objected to, on account of Israel &
his family—They are imprisoned 3 days
—The brethren reason concerning their
cruelty to Joseph, and consider all this as
the hand of God upon them—Simeon bound
and cast into prison—The rest set out on
their journey—They are surprised at finding their money returned in their sacks—
They arrive in Canaan, and relate to their
father all that befell them in Egypt—Long
discourse between Jacob and them, upon
their present circumstances—They per-
suade Jacob to send Benjamin along with
them—Jacob favoured with a divine
vision, and is comforted.

B O O K VI.

PHARAOH had such proofs daily of Joseph's wisdom and fidelity, that he fixed no limits to his power; whatever was done throughout the land of Egypt, he was the doer of it, and whatever he did prospered in his hand. His equipage was next in grandeur to that of his majesty himself, and only in the throne was Pharaoh greater than he. He went through the whole kingdom, provided granaries, appointed deputies in every province for purchasing of all sorts of grain, the advantage of which was afterwards found not only by the Egyptians but other kingdoms adjacent.

As his duty and pleasure run in the same channel, he collected corn sufficient, during the seven years of plenty,

to

to fupply the Egyptian empire for twice feven years of famine, had it been the pleafure of God to continue it fo long ; and this he was prompted to by his native benevolence, that thereby he might affift other diftreffed ftates. Never was a perfon more venerated than Jofeph was by the Egyptians, when they faw every thing come to pafs according to his prediction. All held him to be a peculiar favourite of the Gods, and many of the vulgar could not help believing him to be fome celeftial deity, come down in human form to be the preferver of their beloved nation. For the Egyptians were under no doubt at all, that they were the people moft dear to heaven. What different treatment did Elijah meet with from the feed of Ifrael, when he foretold the famine that fell out in his days ? He was accounted the troubler of Ifrael, and was glad to fly for his life.

Jofeph had continued to purchafe corn for the fpace of feven years ; but fuch was now the will of Providence, that the rains fell not at their feafon

upon

upon the mountains of Abyſſinia, in their uſual quantity, to feed the ſtreams of the Nile.   So that the waters meaſured not above ſeven cubits upon the Nileſcope.   A quantity ſcarce ſufficient to water the very loweſt parts of the country.   Of courſe there was very little grain produced in any part of the land, and that which grew was like Pharaoh's thin ears, not worth the reaping. Now the famine began ſenſibly to be felt in the land of Canaan ; and the Egyptians applied in their turn to their provident governor, to purchaſe food for their families.

The aged patriarch ſeeing the approach of pale hunger towards his famɪly, made diligent enquiry where food might be procured for money ; and being informed that in Egypt only there was corn.   He aſſembled his deſcendants, and thus addreſſed them.   " You ſee my ſons, that the allwiſe Governor provoked by the ſins of men, has denied the firſt and latter rains in their ſeaſon.   Thoſe lofty ſeas which ride upon the air, are not ſuffered to deſcend

and

and vifit the thirfty world. You fee
there is neither earing nor harveft in
the land, our family provifion is almoft
exhaufted, and ghaftly famine makes
hafty ftrides towards the dwelling of Ifrael.   But why ftand we gazing fear-
fully at one another ? Let us ufe the
means of fupport whilft in our power.
We can but die, when the means of life
have forfaken us.   I am informed that
fertile Egypt abounds with provifion,
whilft the reft of the world is ftarving
for want ; and that fo hofpitable is the
governor of that land, that he fends
none away empty who apply unto him
for relief.   Arife therefore my fons,
go down thither, and bring us provifion
for money ; for money will be ufelefs
to us, when the ftaff of bread is cut off.
from our mouths.   Thus fhall ye avoid
feeing your wives and children perifh
for want of fuftenance—Go all of you
except Benjamin.   I defire that he
may be left to fuperintend our domeftic
affairs in your abfence." Benjamin
being all that the patriarch now poffeffed of his dear departed Rachel, he
                                could

could not bear the thoughts of his being expofed to the dangers of fuch a journey.

The fons of Ifrael readily agreed to his propofal, and departed the enfuing morning towards Egypt. Two days before they arrived at the capital, in the dead of the night as they flept in the inn, Simeon dreamed that he was at Dothan along with his brethren confulting the death of Jofeph; which being determined, he thought that juft as they were going to caft him into the pit, an invifible hand was ftretched down from heaven, fnatched Jofeph from the threatning danger, and carried him out of their fight. And as it lifted Jofeph from the earth, with a joftle tumbled Simeon himfelf into the pit defigned for his brother. Alarmed with his danger, he awoke in a fright ere he reached the bottom. Hard as his flinty heart was, the impreffion of this dream made him realize the anxiety of Jofeph's mind on that day of his calamity. Nor could he, notwithftanding his refolution and courage, prevent his heart being dejected

P 2

jeƐted under the apprehenſion that his
dream was ominous of ſome event fatal to his peace. Therefore the reſt of
the journey was dull and unpleaſant to
him.

Joſeph by the ſpirit of prophefy
knew that the famine was extenſive,
and reached even to the land of his
fathers ; and therefore conjeƐtured that
amongſt the many who came for proviſion, his brethren alſo might arrive ;
therefore deſcribed them to his ſteward,
and direƐted him, that if ſuch men
ſhould arrive, that they ſhould not be
ſerved before they were brought before
him. Accordingly when they came,
and applied at the granaries for corn,.
they were direƐted to wait on the governor's ſteward, who told them he could
not poſſibly give them an anſwer till
his maſter, the lord high-chancellor,
came home. But that being only gone
out with his majeſty for an airing, he
would have them abide near the palace
till noon, about which time he expeƐt-
ed his return. They did ſo, and beheld ſuch dazzling ſplendour in the
king's

king's and. Joseph's equipage as they had never seen at any time before.

Brought before Joseph, he imme-diately recollected the features of eve-ry countenance, but they had not the leaft fufpicion of him ; and notwith-ftanding his eminent meeknefs and hu-manity, he could not help the recollec-tion of their bafenefs. The fight of them brought all his fufferings afrefh to his mind. They bow before him with the moft humble reverence, with their faces towards the earth, and wait for him to afk their bufinefs. This brought his dreams alfo to his mind, and with a borrowed fternnefs he demanded their bufinefs with him, and directed his eye chiefly to Simeon.

Judah replied, for he was fpeaker at this time for the reft. "May it pleafe your excellency, we are from the land of Canaan. Being preffed with the fa-mine in our native country, hearing that there was plenty of corn in Egypt, and alfo the fame of the governor's hof-pitality, we were induced to come down to purchafe a little food for ourfelves,

our

our wives and children, that they perifh not in the general fcarcity."

"Tell me not, faid he with a menacing countenance, of fuch men as you being concerned in traffic. There is fomething in each of you that befpeaks you fprung from no common race ; for by your deportment you might be the fons of a king. I fufpect you to be men of birth, fervants of fome martial, enterprifing ftate, come under this difguife to fpy out the nakednefs of the land."

"No my lord, returned the parent of the Jews. We are no fpies, but true men ; by the nakednefs of our own country, forced to feek for provifion in a land more bleffed with the bounties of Providence. We are ftrangers to court intrigue, and have no concern in martial atchievements. Whatever may be the appearances of our perfons, your excellency may affure yourfelf that all our concern has been about cattle from our infancy. For your fervants are not courtiers but fimple fhepherds, and our only bufinefs in Egypt is to procure
food

food for our families; for which we are very willing to pay whatever my lord may demand."

" No, no, returned Joseph, such men as you have not the appearance of shepherds. Nor does your eloquence my friend discover you to be an attendant on the bleating herd. You would not be proper agents for carrying on a treacherous design against our state, if you had not sagacity to cover it over with dissimulation and guile. I tell you, you are spies, come with a bad design against the state."

" Far be it my lord, said Judah, from your servants to be guilty of the dissimulation that your Excellency speaks of. I assure you that we are all shepherds, as our fathers for some generations backward have been. We are the descendants of Abraham, whose name perhaps your excellency has heard of. We ten are brethren; sons of one man in the land of Canaan. One remains this day with our father, and the other, alas ! is not now numbered among his brethren."

" Well

" Well, replied Joſeph, ye declare your innocence in point of treachery. But I ſhall not take your bare word for it, but will prove you, and if ye bear the trial and approve yourſelves to be true men and no ſpies, you ſhall find in me a friend : and you ſhall have liberty to go and come at your pleaſure, and traffic in all the coaſts of Egypt ; but if it is found that ye are traitors and ſpies, ye ſhall ſurely be put to death.— By this ſhall you prove yourſelves to be honeſt men. Let one of you be diſpatched to your father's houſe and fetch that younger brother of whom you ſpeak, and then will it appear that your words are right. If you refuſe this, it is a ſign that your purpoſe is bad, and as ſure as Pharaoh lives ye are ſpies upon our ſtate."

" No, my lord we are not ſpies indeed, anſwered Judah with a ſubmiſſive voice, notwithſtanding we have one reaſon wherefore we cannot with pleaſure ſubmit to your excellency's command. And that is not fear of being detected as ſpies ; but the famine of

our

our houfes. For we left but barely fufficient to fupply the wants of our wives and children, during the time neceffary for us to come hither for food, and return again unto them. If we fhould do as my lord hath faid, then muft all our father's houfe perifh for want in our abfence, and we fhould be guilty of their blood. Wherefore if nothing but that will fatisfy your excellency of our fidelity, it is better for us to fubmit to death in a ftrange land, than to return and be witneffes of the evil to come on our deareft kindred; for we cannot furvive the deftruction of our father's houfe."

Jofeph commanded his guards in waiting to take the ten brethren into cuftody and carry them to prifon, where he kept them three days and three nights; but withal he gave fecret orders to his ftewards to look well to them, to their fervants and cattle, that they fhould lack nothing. On the third morning, as foon as the fun enlightened the earth he ordered them all before him, and thus he addreffed them. " I

have

have confidered all that you have faid,
when you were laft before me ; and as
there is a poffibility of your teftimony
being true, I would not expofe your old
father of whom ye fpake, nor your
wives and little ones, to the feverity of
famine ; for I fear God, and am no
ftranger to the feelings of humanity.—
One condition I propofe to you, which
muft and fhall be complied with, and
that is, one of you fhall be left bound
in the houfe of your prifon, as an hoftage to enfure your return ; and all the
reft of you fhall go to your families,
with what provifion you can carry, and
when ye come again be fure you bring
your younger brother along with you.
Which if you do, your hoftage fhall be
delivered up to you, and you fhall all go
in peace again to your father. But if
you return not, he who I fhall fecure
as an hoftage fhall pay for your unfaith-
fulnefs with his life."

"O faid Judah, how doth one fin
bring a lafting train of evils after it ?
Er and Onan are fallen victims to that
juftice which avengeth Jofeph's afflictions

tions. Another is now demanded, and who knows what the issue will be ? The guilt of our brother's blood pursues us, and embitter's every Providence. Our God leaves us to intreat in vain ; because when we saw the anguish of his afflicted soul, we would shew him no mercy, although he besought us with tears. Lord, thy conduct is just, we alone are guilty."

" Did not I, said Reuben, do what I could to dissuade you from a deed so vile and barbarous ? I used every argument, I was master of, to prevail with you to save the child's life, but all in vain. And with a view to be able to restore him to his father's embrace, I proposed his being let down into the pit, and had performed my purpose the ensuing night, had I not been prevented by your untimely sale of him to strangers, who have carried him I know not whither. But the all-seeing and ever watchful Providence, I doubt not shelters him from injury in some country more hospitable, and affords him that peace and pleasure which he was deni-

Q   ed

ed in the houfe of his brethren, whilft we, his perfecutors, are juftly purfued by the avenging hand of Jofeph's God."

" I freely confefs, faid Simeon, that I never felt a proper remorfe for that fin againft my brother till five nights ago, when I realized the anguifh of his foul in what I myfelf felt in my dream. And from what I then felt, I have reafon to fear that fomething of a very afflicting nature is before me, for I found myfelf exactly in Jofeph's circumftances when he was laft in the pit ; fince then my mind has never been free from either the diftreffing idea of the boy's anxiety, or the overwhelming grief of our poor father, when Levi and I prefented the bloody coat to him at Mamre. But let what will come, I find I deferve it. I fhould wifh to be as fubmiffive in my affliction, as I was refolute in perpetrating the guilty deed."

Little did the fons of Jacob imagine, that the lord high-chancellor underftood their difcourfe, for the better to conceal his relation to them, he had fpoken all along by an interpreter, whom he caufed

to

to withdraw as foon as his brethren began to confer among themfelves. With
all the diftance that Jofeph affected,
with all the refolution he could fummon
up, he found that he could not fupprefs
the rifing tide of fraternal fympathy,
ready to gufh from his eyes upon hearing his brethrens' penitent conference ;
therefore he turned him into a private
apartment, and gave free vent to the e-
motions of his manly heart. And as
foon as he had compofed himfelf he returned to them into the hàll, and com-
muned with them about the affairs of
their native country, till their facks
were filled and their camels and affes
loaded with corn. But never was there
fuch a ftruggle between found policy
and brotherly tendernefs, as Jofeph felt
in his difturbed mind. Brotherly love
urged him to fly to the embraces of his
brethren, but found policy advifed to
ftay his careffes, till he had proved their
regard to Benjamin his brother. Sound
policy will prevail over paffion, where
wifdom prefides.

It was juft as Simeon's foreboding
heart had prefaged, for Jofeph felected

him from amongft his brethren, to detain him as an hoftage for the return of
the reft ; although it went now againft
the tendernefs of his inclination to give
pain even to Simeon, fince he had fome
proof of his penitence. But he found
himfelf under a neceffity of either detain-
ing one or difcovering himfelf to them;
the latter of which he chofe not to do
for the prefent. Simeon therefore was
bound in the prefence of his brethren,
and conveyed to prifon : whilft the reft
were difmiffed from the prefence of Jofeph, and began their journey towards
Canaan. Not without much reflection
upon the calamity to which they were
reduced, and their cruelty to Jofeph as
the procuring caufe of all.

Arrived at the inn, how great was
their furprife, when Iffachar opening
his fack to give his afs provender, found
all the money he had given for his corn
returned in the mouth of it ; aftonifhed
at the event, he tells his brethren. E-
qually aftonifhed, they fly every man to
his fack to examine, and lo ! in the mouth
of every man's fack is found his money
in

'in full tale.   In filent amazement they
look at one another.   Every one knows
himfelf to have been clear ; but no one
'man could be certain about his fellows.
All alledged that the hand of their God
was upon them for evil ; but no one
could fo much as conjecture how their
money fhould come to be returned.—
Sleep departed from the eyes of the pa-
triarchs that night, for they expected
every moment to hear the voice of the
purfuers, coming to carry them back to
the governor.   In fhort, at laft they confidered the matter as a fraud put upon
them, to find a pretext to enflave them.
And well knowing that their detention
in Egypt would prove the deftruction of
the houfe of Jacob, they refolved not to
fubmit tamely to their betrayers, but to
perifh on the fpot rather than be flaves
to fuch perfidy, and to fell their lives as
dear as poffible.   Now they lament the
abfence of Simeon, the ftrength of whofe
brawny arm they had heretofore amply
proved.   But all in vain their fears, and
vain their defperate purpofes.   For Jofeph had fecretly commanded his chief

Q 2   factor ·

factor to return all their money into their feveral facks, in the fame order which it was found ; fo that when morning came, none appeared in purfuit of them. They laded their cattle and proceeded on their journey, every now and then looking behind them to fee if any danger appeared ; and thus they proceeded from day to day, till they arrived at their own habitations.

The good old patriarch looking out, faw them at a diftance moving on heavily, becaufe of their loads of provifion. And how did his aged heart beat thick with joy to fee them fafely returned with food for their families ? but how foon did his joy abate, when he difcovered that Simeon was miffing ? They found themfelves under a neceffity of declaring all that had paft, between the governor of Egypt and them in their abfence, and that Benjamin was demanded. Upon hearing of which the good man's heart failed him, and he could not forbear thus chiding them for their conduct. " Could not you, men of your years, never remarkable for ignorance,

rance, have gone and bought provifion. for us, without revealing the circum-ftances of your family ? What need was there for you to have mentioned that you had another brother at all ? That could be nothing to a foreigner, nor would it have been at all enquired into, if you had not incautioufly mentioned it. I cannot agree that Benjamin fhould go. On your account I am bereaved of my Jofeph. You have no more mercy on my feeble age, than to take Benjamin away alfo. All thefe things are againft me."

Reuben, the elder born, approached and refpectfully anfwered his father, " Were we infenfible of the grief and affliction of a parent fo venerable, we fhould debafe ourfelves below brutality itfelf. Let not Ifrael charge us with want of tender regard, if we have thro' the neceffity of circumftances been induced to declare, what he could wifh to have been concealed. For my own part, I am of opinion that the governor's countenance muft greatly belye his heart if any evil is to be apprehended at his hand.

hand. There is something so amiable
and attractive in him, that I think I
could without hesitation entrust my
life in his hand. And as a proof of my
sincerity, I offer, that if my father will
permit Benjamin to go along with his
brethren as we have engaged, to leave
my two sons Hanoch and Phallu as
pledges for his return ; and if any harm
befal him, let them be slain."

"Ah Reuben ! replied the aged man,
thou talkest in a simple stile. Should
Benjamin be lost, the death of my grand-
sons would but make the wound deeper
and more painful. Joseph is already
dead, Benjamin is all that is now left of
Rachel, for whom I served your grandfather fourteen years ; and should he go
with you, and evil befal him as it did
Joseph, this hoary head would come
down with an insupportable load of sorrow to the grave. My son Benjamin
shall not go down with you."

Aged Jacob soon perceiving that
their late purchase was three-fourths
expended, apprized his sons of the necessity of returning into Egypt to re-
new

new their ſtock of proviſions, to prevent the devaſtations which meagre famine would otherwiſe make in their dwellings. " Go, ſaid he, my ſons, return into Egypt and buy us a little more food for the houſhold." " We go, Sir, replied Judah, if Benjamin go with us ; but if he is not with us, we cannot go : for the lord-chancellor ſolemnly proteſted to us that unleſs we brought our youngeſt brother with us, we ſhould. not ſee his face ; and that if we did bring him, we ſhould, under the ſhadow of his protection, have full liberty to. traffic in any part of Egypt. Think, therefore, my father, what we are to do, for want will ſpeedily be here."

The holy man, with an heart wrung with ſorrow, replied, " Wherefore, Judah, dealt ye ſo ill with me, as to tell the lord of the land that you had another brother, for I underſtand that you was ſpeaker for your brethren ?"

" Alas, Sir ! the man was very ſtrict in examining of us concerning our ſtate, our kindred, the number of our father's children ; and we told him the truth

truth in every thing. Could we certainly know that he would demand our brother of us ? And had we known that he would say bring your brother down to me ; we durst not have diffembled and uttered falfhood, for then we fhould have offended our God ; and you yourfelf would have grieved for our tranfgreffion. Allow me to fay that my worthy father errs in his over-carefulnefs for Benjamin. We are all your fons as well as he ; therefore equally intitled to your tender regard. But Simeon lies in chains, in a foreign land, pale famine ftares you and all of us, our wives and little ones in the face. Nothing can fave the life of Simeon, but our return into Egypt with our brother Benjamin : and nothing can fave our tender families at home, but fpeedy fupplies from that county. Send him with me my father. I will be furety for him, of my hand do you require him. If you will fend him, we will arife and go directly ; but if not, we cannot go. We may as well ftay at home and die by famine, with our wives, and little

ones,

ones, as be put to the fword in a ftrange land. Determine, therefore, what we are to do, my father. For unlefs we had thus lingered, we might have been all fafely returned the fecond time.—— And let Ifrael confider that certain death awaits us all, if Benjamin is not permitted to go with us, and there is but a bare peradventure of danger to him if he goes. Remember, my father, the God of Bethel, in whom thou haft trufted, he is in Egypt as well as in Canaan. He is able to protect thy Benjamin in what land foéver."

He ended here, and the penfive patriarch replied. " Well, Judah, your reafoning is home and conclufive. We will call the boy and enquire at his own mouth : if he is willing, I fhall not further oppofe his going ; but if he is not willing, I will by no means conftrain him. Are you willing, Benjamin, to accompany your brethren through the dangers of another journey to Egypt ? They proteft they will not go without you, and I am very unwilling to expofe your young and tender years to the

the hardſhips and dangers of ſuch a journey. Be free my ſon, and ſpeak your mind ?" Said Benjamin, " I ſhould ill deſerve to call Jacob my father, if I ſhould ſo much as deſire to ſhun any dangers to which my brethren are expoſed. Far be it from me to delight in loitering at home, whilſt they by hardſhip and toil are caring for me and my little ones. I am not only perfectly willing to go with them, my father, but even deſirous of it ; and would have propoſed it ere now, had it not been for fear of adding to your burden, my father ; I want to ſee this lord-governor of Egypt. I know not how it is : but ever ſince my brother Reuben gave you an account of him, I have found my mind unaccountably attached to him. And laſt night I dreamed that I ſtood in his preſence along with my brethren, and I thought I ſaw ſomething ſo unſpeakably agreeable in him, that I could not but love him. But when he came to embrace me (for I thought he embraced me) I felt ſuch a glow of friendſhip warm my

boſom,

bosom, that I never experienced the like
in my life. For my part, I am of Reuben's mind, I fear no harm from lord-
governor."—" Well, my son, said the
hoary patriarch, with a deep groan, I
must submit. God grant that you be
not mistaken in the man."

" But, my sons, take double money
along with you, besides that which was
returned in your sacks and repay it ;
perhaps it might be done undesignedly
by some of the overseers of the stores.
And go not empty handed to the man,
seeing a gift in the bosom pacifieth anger, but take with you an handsome
present of the best produce of our land :
such as balm, honey, spices, myrrh, nuts
and almonds. And, O God Almighty,
go thou with my sons, and give them
favour in the sight of the governor."

The sons of Israel departed ; the
Lord appeared unto Jacob, in a vision
of the night, and said unto him, " Jacob, what seest thou ?" Jacob replied,
" I see an almond tree, exceeding fair,
smooth and strong in the trunk, branch-
ed out into twelve capital boughs, each

R   of

of which are fubdivided into innumerable branches, and all laden with fruit of the moft luxuriant growth." The vifion anfwered, " Thou haft well feen, Jacob. Thou art the beautiful almond tree, from thee twelve branches are fprung, which fhall bring forth feed innumerable as the fand of the fea. Afk not how it can be done, feeing one branch is lopped off from the native ftem. Be fatisfied in this, that what infinite wifdom hath purpofed, almighty power can accomplifh ; leave thy Benjamin to the care of his God, for thou fhalt embrace him in fafety." So fpake the vifion, and departing left a glow of feraphic fervour in the patriarch's heart, fomething like that which he felt at Peniel, when like a prince, he prevailed with God.

T H E

THE

LIFE

OF

JOSEPH.

ARGUMENT.

The sons of Israel arrive at Memphis with Benjamin—Judah apologiseth for the returned money—Offers the present Jacob had sent—They are invited to dine with the governor—Their jealousy of some design against them—Simeon's opinion is asked—Their meeting with Joseph—His struggle with natural affection—They dine with him—His scheme to try their affection to Benjamin—They are pursued by the steward—Searched, and Benjamin is convicted of stealing Joseph's cup—They all return to the palace—Judah confesseth their former guilt—Levi's lamentation for Benjamin—Judah's defence for Benjamin—Benjamin studieth to reconcile his brethren to his fate—Simeon and Levi resolve to rescue him or die with him—Joseph makes himself known to his brethren—He comforts and encourages them—Invites them and all his father's house to come to live in Egypt—They regale themselves with Joseph and depart from Egypt.

BOOK VII.

ARRIVED in Egypt, they were conducted into the governor's presence, who inwardly rejoiced to see the sons of his father safely returned in company with Benjamin his brother.—— "Well said he, you have fulfilled the condition on your part, it behoves me to be equally faithful on mine ; I shall give orders for your brother's immediate release from prison." When he saw them all together, he ordered his steward to kill a killing, and make plentiful provision ; for said he, these men shall be my guests to-day. Having given necessary orders for his houshold affairs, and having business to dispatch abroad, he left his brethren alone until noon. Now Judah approached the steward, and thus apologized for the

money

money that was returned in their facks. " O my lord, we are under great difficulty at prefent, and have need of your friendfhip, as your influence with my lord the chancellor is great. When we came down at firft, notwithftanding your lord was jealous of us, we had indeed no other bufinefs in Egypt but to buy food for our families. The corn we purchafed and as we thought paid for, but to our great furprife and grief, when we opened our facks every man found his money in full weight in the mouth of his fack. How it came there we cannot conceive. But willing to deal uprightly with all men, we have brought that money which was returned, again in our hand, befides the money which we would now lay out for frefh provifion. Will it pleafe my lord to accept the returned money, and pardon what overfight foever might occafion it ? We have alfo brought a fmall prefent, of the fruits of our land, for my lord the chancellor, which we beg you would prefent to him in our name."

" Your prefent for my lord, faid the

ſteward.

steward, I willingly accept for him :. but as for your money, I cannot receive it : as you paid the full value when you received your corn. As to the money ye found in your facks, make your-selves very eafy about it. It is a gift of your God, from which no evil is like-ly to enfue. Set your hearts at reft, and compofe yourfelves, for I have or-ders from my lord to inform you, that he expects you all to dine with him at. noon in his palace." As they did not. much relifh this invitation, they would gladly have excufed themfelves from the honour defigned, and with more peaceful thoughts have dined on an humble allowance in their inn ; but as no excufe could be admitted, they were obliged to fubmit to the governor's pleafure.

The steward withdrawn, and they left alone, they began thus to reafon one with another. One faid, "Simeon's releafe looks well upon the governor's fide, but I like not this invitation.— There is oftentimes the moft malignant defign carried on under the mafk of friendfhip.

friendſhip. Now we have convinced him that we are no ſpies, ſaid another, I fear he is about deviſing ſome other plauſible preſence to detain us as ſlaves in the land. I muſt confeſs ſaid a third, that an invitation to ſuch as we, to dine with the ſecond perſon of the empire, looks very dubious. For my part, ſaid young Benjamin, I am under no apprehenſion of any ſuch thing ; I ſee ſomething in my lord-chancellor, that convinceth me that it is impoſſible for him to allow himſelf in unrighteouſneſs.—— What is your opinion, Simeon ? You have had more acquaintance with the Egyptian manners than we have had."

"Really, my brother, ſaid Simeon, I know not what to think of the preſent invitation, any more than the reſt of you. To me it muſt ſeem ſomewhat myſterious, to be brought from a priſon to dine in a palace. Yet I aſſure you, I met with no ill-uſage here, further than my confinement. I was bound you ſaw in your preſence, but as ſoon as you were departed, I was led away to an apartment agreeable in all reſpects,

spects, except that I was confined to it.
—I was daily supplied with plenty of
excellent food, but from whence it
came, I was never informed. The governor himself did me the honour of frequent visits, and conversed familiarly
with me concerning the Hebrew lineage, (for he appears to be no stranger
to Abraham, notwithstanding he is an
Egyptian) concerning our father, and
Benjamin, and especially concerning
the death of Joseph; and I have ob-
served, that when we have been con-
versing about these things, sometimes
the tears would steal involuntarily from
his eyes. I cannot say that I have any
apprehension of evil, now you have fulfilled your engagements."

As they were thus reasoning among
themselves, Joseph came home and ordered them into the hall of his palace.
The steward at their request, presented
the balm, myrrh, &c. which he received with visible satisfaction, to the great
pleasure of his brethren. Then ordered
them all to sit down, and enquired after their welfare.

"" Have

" Have you been all well, my friends
faid he, fince your departure hence ?
Did you find your good old father a-
live and well ? Are your wives and children well ?

Judah replied, " We got well home,
and found thy fervant our father in as
good health as his advanced age would
permit, likewife our wives and children
we found well. But we have caufe to
fear for our father at our return, for it
cut him to the heart to part with his
youngeft fon."

" And this is your younger brother
of whom ye fpake ! faid he, God be gracious to thee my fon. I hope thy father
will have no caufe to be forrowful for
fending thee hither."

He faid, but his fwollen heart could
bear no more. He knew not how to
keep from his brother's embrace. Therefore he hafted from the hall, before his
brethren fhould perceive his diforder,
and fought a private apartment, where
he might give vent to the overflowings
of his heart. But that he would prove
them whether they retained the fame
malignant

malignant difpofition towards Benjamin
that they had done towards him, he
would have rufhed to their embrace
and bedewed them with fraternal tears.
But, as before, his wifdom fuperfeded
his paffion, and he concealed his affection for them till he could be fatisfied
of their temper towards Benjamin.

Having eafed his almoft burfted
bofom, by the briny flood he fhed, he
wafhed off the tears from his face, went
into dinner with the fons of his father,
who all fat at table with him according
to feniority, from Reuben down to Benjamin. Thus feated, Jofeph fent mef-
fes from before him unto them all, beginning at Benjamin and leaving off at
Levi, of whofe repentance he had no
particular proof. But little Benjamin's
mefs was a five fold portion, defigned
to inform him that he had found a friend
in the governor of Egypt. So they eat
and drank till they were merry in his
prefence.

But Jofeph, in order to prove their
regard to his brother Benjamin, contrived to have him arrefted as an offender,

der, to fee what an effect it would have
upon them. Accordingly he commanded his fteward, faying, "I have
not yet done with thefe men, I muft
get you to affift me in a fcheme which
I have devifed to put them to a more
clofe trial than before. Go fill their
facks with corn, and put every man's
money in the mouth of his fack, and
take this filver cup of mine, and put it
into that of the youngeft, along with his
corn money. But do it yourfelf, let
none be privy to it but you and I."

They had not been long departed,
before the fteward was commanded to
take a troop of light horfe and purfue
them, charge them with the theft, and
bring them back unto the governor.——
Great was their furprife when they
looked behind them and faw a company of armed men clofely purfuing them.
They ftopped their cattle and ftood ftill
to enquire the caufe. "Is this, faid
the fteward, the manner in which ye
foreigners requite the kindnefs of my
lord? Could not you partake of his hof-
pitality, without ftealing away his plate.

You

You are poffeffed of my lord's cup, the filver cup out of which my lord drinketh, and whereby indeed he divineth. This is bafely done to requite his goodnefs to you with fuch evil."

"I am amazed, faid Judah, to hear fuch a charge from the mouth of my lord. God forbid that any of the fons of Ifrael fhould be guilty of fuch bafenefs. Confider, Sir, how unlikely it is that we fhould be guilty of ftealing your lord's cup. When our money was returned in our facks unknown to us, we brought it back from the land of Canaan. Had we been difhoneftly inclined, why kept we it not to ourfelves? How then fhould we go to fteal from thy mafter either filver or gold? But you are welcome to fearch and fatisfy yourfelf. And if it be found with us, he with whom it is found fhall die, and the reft of us will be content to become bondmen to your mafter."

"Be it fo, replied the fteward, he with whom the cup is found fhall be detained a bondman to my mafter, but all the reft may proceed on their journey.

S

ney.

ney. They hafted and unladed their
cattle, and the fteward began to fearch
beginning at the facks of the eldeft till
he came to Benjamin's fack, out of
which to their utter confufion he took
his mafter's filver cup, in the prefence
of them all, held it up, and faid, "Are
you now wrongfully charged ?" In utter defpair they rent their clothes, laded their cattle and returned to the city,
for they would not go forward without
their brother Benjamin.

Jofeph was ftill in the hall waiting
their return, and had collected all the
fternnefs he was mafter of, into his
countenance. " What is this, faid
he, that you have done : Did you fuppofe that I could not find out your
treachery ? Is it right in you thus to requite kindnefs ?"

They all fell proftrate before him,
with their faces to the earth, and Judah with humble fubmiffion thus addreffed him : "Alas ! my lord, it will be
in vain for us to proteft our innocence,
feeing the cup was found in our poffeffion: Though the God of governors
                                will

will not charge us with putting it there. It is not for this, but old iniquity, for which thy fervants fuffer. It is not thy hand, but that of our God that is upon us. We confefs his judgments to be juft. We fubmit to his fentence, and yield ourfelves bondmen in a ftrange land. Take us, my lord, and difpofe of us as you pleafe. Farewell aged and honourable Ifrael, may Abraham's God be thy divine fupport, for thou feeft thy fons no more forever. Jofeph is not, Benjamin is convicted of felony, and all thy fons are determined not to furvive his fate. He fhall not bear the guilt of his brethren alone. Farewell, beloved wives and tender prattling infants, no more you fly to the glowing embraces of your hufbands and parents ! Injured, Jofeph ! never did the blood of Abel cry louder for vengeance, than thine doth ! Er and Onan are both already fallen victims to avenge thee.—— And now all the race of Jacob are required. Innocent Benjamin, why fhould he fuffer with his guilty brethren ?" So faying, his voice was ftopped by his rif-

ing

ing forrow, and he poured forth a flood of repentant and grieffull tears ; and then proceeded : " Keep us not in fufpenfe, my lord. Let us know our doom, for we are prepared to meet the worft."

"God forbid that I fhould do injuftice to you, faid Jofeph, in either putting you to death, or keeping you all for bondmen. Only he with whom the cup was found fhall be liable to punifhment. And as for the reft of you, go ye home to your father in peace : and come and traffic in the land, whenever you have occafion. There is a law of certain and punctual equity, which ought to be obferved by all in power ; and that is on the one hand, not to let the offender pafs with impunity ; nor on the other, to punifh the innocent however nearly allied to the guilty. I fear God. His law is my rule, it warrants me to punifh delinquency wherever it is found ; but forbids me at all to opprefs the innocent. You ten are therefore at liberty to go where you will, my bufinefs is alone with the offender."

"Alas ! my brother Benjamin, faid
Levi ;

Levi ; is all your prepoſſeſſion in favour
of the governor come to this ? How was
thy ſimple and honeſt heart beguiled ?
O my brother, how deluſive was thy
dream that made, as thou thought, the
governor's friendly embrace thrill with
a warming glow throughout thy whole
boſom ? Oh my brother, my brother !
I ſhall never return to Canaan without
thee."

Judah came forward, and thus implored the chancellor's mercy. "Alas!
my lord ; ſpare the young man, our brother, from bonds, impriſonment, and
death. But for the guilt of his brethren,
his birth might ſeem to have promiſed
better profpects. Much might be urged in our brother's defence. He is
young, inexperienced, and has ſeen
but little of the world. His conduct
has hitherto been unimpeached ; and
merciful governors do not uſually pun-
iſh with ſeverity the firſt fault of any
delinquent. It might be urged that the
lad was not preſent when the ſacks were
filled ; and there is at leaſt a poſſibility
of the cup being conveyed into his

ſack

fack without his knowledge. Never-
theleſs, as appearances are ſtrong a-
gainſt him, we ſtand not to juſtify
ourſelves but rely upon the clemency
of my lord governor. Although the
guilt may be charged but upon one, the
puniſhment muſt of neceſſity fall upon
the whole ; for our fate is involved in
his. Allow me to ſay it, for I now
ſpeak for life or death, that mercy is
the brighteſt perfection of Deity, and
muſt therefore be the glory of princes
and governors : anger and reſentment
being paſſions fitted only for ſlaves and
narrow contracted ſelfiſh ſpirits. We
have here delivered up ourſelves to
your lordſhip, and I think it would not
be for the honor of Egypt, for its governor to deſtroy a number of men,
who are willing to become indebted
for their lives to his mercy and favour.
You have already relieved us when we
otherwiſe muſt have periſhed for want ?
be pleaſed to exerciſe the ſame clemency in beſtowing a free pardon upon
theſe that are willing to be accounted
guilty. What if the God of our fathers
whoſe

whofe wifdom is unfearchable, and whofe judgments are a great deep, fhould have fuffered your fervants to fall into thefe diftreffing circumftances, on purpofe to furnifh my lord with further opportunity of exercifing his virtue. It will indeed fhew a noble difpofition in my lord governor, to delight in conferring life and mercy, rather than in taking ftrict vengeance for injuries fuftained by himfelf.

" Let my lord affure himfelf, that it is not for our own life and fafety that we are thus folicitous. No, life has loft its principal charms, fince fuch a reproach is brought upon the houfe of Ifrael. But it is tendernefs for a good old father, already bowed down with a feries of adverfe providences. And the lofs of his children will bring down his honourable grey hairs with forrow to the grave. I know well what I fay, my lord. I have felt the wringings of parental anguifh on the fudden lofs of my own children. I have feen the infupportable forrow of my father's fpirit upon the lofs of his Jofeph. And

fhould

should he be bereaved of Benjamin, in whom his very life is wrapt up, it is eaſy to ſee what will follow. Perhaps, my lord, has an aged father alive. Suppoſe him, my lord, in the place of our father, and let his hoary hairs be an advocate for an unhappy youth, whoſe life is in your hand. You have ſons, my lord. From your parental tenderneſs to them, conceive what our father muſt feel upon the loſs of his children. —There is ſomething ſacred in the name of father, therefore the Moſt High hath choſen it, as one of the endearing names whereby he reveals himſelf to his people, and whereby he chooſeth to be addreſſed by them. God your heavenly father, will certainly requite all the kindneſs which you ſhall ſhew to this young man, and unto us in him. I pray, my lord, by all that is tender and endearing in the bonds of nature : by all that is amiable in a member of ſociety, and by the endearing obligations we are all under to the Father of Mercies, that you will ſpare the boy to be a comfort to his aged parent."

"I

" I became bound to reftore him to his father again, and fhall not return without him. If he is to die, I offer myfelf in his ftead. Or if the fentence is flavery, it is the fame. Death and flavery are alike to me. In faying this, I fpeak but the fentiments of all my brethren, for they are all determined to ftand or fall with Benjamin."

So faying he caft himfelf at the governor's feet, and all the reft after him in joint mediation for their unhappy brother. All feemingly to no purpofe.

Benjamin with an amiable ferenity, and with a glow of brotherly affection, faid, " My brethren, if the governor's heart is a ftranger to pity, I fear not what he can inflict. It is but to die, and he himfelf cannot efcape it. But live ye, my brethren, for Ifrael's fake accept the life that is offered to you.— It will be fome fatisfaction for our good father to hear that his Benjamin is innocent of the crime for which he fuffers. Let me repeat my requeft, my brethren, for I fear not death."

With the greateft difficulty, Jofeph fuppreffed

fuppreffed the guft of tender affection
ready to burft forth fo far as to be a-
ble with fome degree of aufterity, to
command the guard to fecure the prifoner.

Simeon and Levi fprung from their
places, drew their well tried fwords,
rufhed between the guards and their
brother, and with all the vehemence
of paffion, cried out, " If Benjamin
dies, he dies neither alone nor unre-
venged. Thefe fwords have been bathed in the blood of hundreds, and hundreds yet fhall perifh ere Benjamin dies,
an unmerited death. The children of
Ham, fhed not Hebrew blood at free
coft. If we muft die, let us fell our
lives as dear as poffible." ,

" Stay your hands upon both fides,
cried Jofeph, it is enough ; let all depart the hall except the eleven brethren
faid he, and all departed: Left alone
with his brethren, Jofeph faid, I have
tried and proved fyour virtue, my brethren and rejoice to fee it. I am Jofeph, your own brother Jofeph." He
faid, and burft into tears as he fell upon

on Benjamin's bofom, and wept aloud, that even the Egyptians heard him.—— His brethren ftood in the utmoft amazement, and confufion glowed upon every countenance. The fight of their injured brother realized all the horrors of their guilt. They durft not approach him, however much they rejoiced at feeing him alive.

He went to them one by one, and embraced them with ardent affection, and in particular he affured Simeon and Levi that their generous valor in defence of his brother Benjamin, had effectually obliterated the laft remains of his refentment, of their former conduct towards him.

When paffion had fubfided on both fides, and cooler reafon had refumed her government, all being feated in the hall of the palace, Jofeph thus harangued them.

" My dear brethren, it is impoffible for me to defcribe the pleafure you have this day given me, by your firm and zealous attachment to Benjamin your brother and mine. It was not without
some

some ground, as you know, that I had
suspicion of your regard to the descendants of my mother Rachel.   To be sat-
isfied in this, I devised the scheme
by which your virtue has so eminently
discovered itself.   Reuben, you deserve
my warmest acknowledgment for the
service you intended me at Dothan ;
but it had been worse for us all to-day,
if your well-meant scheme had succeeded.   Whilst I was in the pit, I had a
vision of an heavenly messenger that informed me of the mind and will of God
concerning me, and perfectly reconciled me to my fate.   Methinks the countenances of Simeon and Levi, are not
free from cloudy apprehensions.   O
my brethren, dismiss your fears.   I
should be worse than an infidel, if your
generous attachment to Benjamin did
not wholly rivet you in my esteem.——
Yes, my brethren, I will ever confide
in the noble resolution of Simeon and
Levi.   I have seen so much of the hand
of my God in my personal affairs, that
I have really lost sight of second caus-
es ; or I love them with the greater

tenderness

tenderness, knowing that there muſt be poignant remorſe following after evil meanings. Your meaning was then evil I acknowledge, but the deſign of God was good. And I ſhould be exceeding culpable before God, if I did not heartily approve of the means by which he has exalted me.

I aſſure you, my brethren, that all paſt injuries are with me, as if they had never been; and I rejoice to ſee the ſpirit of Abraham, Iſaac and Jacob diffuſe itſelf throughout all his ſeed.— Here in this cup of cordial friendſhip, let us drink an eternal oblivion of paſt injuries. And now my brethren, you ſee what God hath done, but perhaps as yet you know not the cauſe of it. —I am here advanced to power and dignity in Egypt : not for my own ſake, but for yours, and that of my father's houſe, to preſerve much people alive. Two years of the famine are already paſt. Laſt year the Nile did not ariſe to its uſual height, by eight cubits ; and this preſent year, not by twelve cubits. Five years are yet to

T   come,

come, in which there shall be neither earing nor harveft.   As this is the cafe, it may reconcile you to what cannot be recalled, or remedied ; and you may fee that God over-ruled your little prejudices for Ifrael's good.   After you have regaled yourfelves with me a day or two, I would have you return to Jacob my father, and tell him of all things that God hath done for me in the land of Egypt.   How that he hath made me as a father to Pharaoh, and lord over all the land.   Tell him that I invite the whole houfe of Ifrael down to Egypt to fojourn till the famine is over and gone.   And lo, I fend light carriages by you to carry my father, your wives and little ones, and bring them down to me."

By this time it was known in Jofeph's palace, that his brethren were come ; it got wind in the ftreets, and flew like lightning from one ftreet to another, till it had fpread itfelf all over the metropolis. . The inhabitants in general, were in a rapture of joy, and to teftify their regard to the lord-high-chancellor,

chancellor, there were bonfires made in every opening, bells ringing, water-works playing, and every other demon-ftration of joy that thofe ancient times admitted of. And even Pharaoh him-felf rejoiced, to hear of the brethren of his favourite being arrived in Mem-phis.

Now Jofeph command Manaffeh and Ephraim to be brought before him, and prefented them to their eleven uncles; and the far Afenath, greatly rejoiced in having found fuch a num-ber of heroic brethren. Pharaoh com-manded Jofeph to fend fuitable pro-vifions and carriages for Jacob and his children, and from the monarch him-felf to invite him to come to Egypt, and affure him of protection and pro-vifion all the time the famine fhould laft. This the confiderate monarch did, to prevent any envious mind from reflecting on Jofeph, for any kindnefs fhewn to the houfhold of Ifrael.

Having regaled themfelves two days with Jofeph, and feen every thing cu-rious and valuable in the metropolis,

he

he sent them away, after he had given
them friendly advice.

After supper, the evening before
they began their journey, Joseph thus
addressed them, " My dear brethren,
you are now going to visit the best and
most honourable of fathers, to carry
him the unexpected news of having
found his son, who has been so long
lost. You will be prudent enough I
hope, to take care how you divulge
the matter to him ; lest the news of
my life should prove as fatal to him, as
the former news of my death had like-
ly to have done. Let it be done with
caution, and by little and little. In all
probability you will find yourselves under a necessity of disclosing the whole
of the former plot against me, in order
to account for my being yet alive.—
But, my brethren, beware of reflecting
upon each others conduct : remember
that the hand of God was in it. I
sympathize with you, my brother Judah, under the heavy loss of my youthful nephews. But I foresee that Judah
shall yet be great in the house of his
father,

father, and they shall descend from Judah, who are destined to rule. Let all thoughts of past things be forever banished from your minds, and cultivate amongst yourselves the strictest amity and friendship. Whilst you stand by one another, as you all nobly did the other day, by my brother Benjamin, no power on earth shall overcome you ; but if ye should disagree among yourselves, ye would become an easy prey to every enemy.

" Ye depart to-morrow. But let me not send you empty away. You will be pleased to accept of this, as a small token of my regard to the children of my father. So saying, he presented each of them with a goodly sum of money and changes of raiment, but Benjamin's present was three times as valuable as any of the rest : he likewise sent ten beasts of burden, laden with the best things of Egypt, as a present to his honourable father ; and other ten laden with healthful and delicate provision for them all by the way.—

Then

Then he bleſſed them, took his leave of them, and retired to communicate the whole adventure to Aſenath, his beloved conſort.

THE

THE

LIFE

OF

JOSEPH.

ARGUMENT.

The sons of Jacob arrive at Canaan—He enquires after all that befel them in their absence—Judah relates the governor's kindness—Jacob expresseth his thankfulness on their account—Excuseth his backwardness to send Benjamin with them—Simeon confesseth their former treachery to Joseph—Judah informs the patriarch of his being alive—Benjamin confirms his report—Jacob faints, but is recovered by the sight of the waggons—Jacob hesitates about accepting Joseph's invitation—He is encouraged by a vision—They set out for Egypt—He meets with Joseph at Hieropolis—Their exceeding joy and endearing caresses—Joseph presents five of his brethren to the king—They are sent to Goshen—Jacob takes up his lodging in Joseph's palace for a time—presented to the king—Relates Abraham's victory over the four kings—The famine ended—Joseph restores the Egyptians to their estates—Sabrina on her death-bed requests a visit from Joseph, that she might implore his forgiveness—He meets unexpectedly with Alvah in distress, requites his former kindness to himself.

BOOK VIII.

THE venerable patriarch, impatient for his sons return, and solicitous for Benjamin's welfare, stood upon an eminence, near his rural dwelling, with his sanguine eye intently fixed upon the way of Egypt. When he beheld his sons afar off, and as fast as feeble age would admit, he hasted to embrace them. Have my sons, said he in his heart, found favour with the governor of Egypt, that they are safely and timely arrived. Blessed be the God of my fathers, who so graciously has returned you all my sons to my longing embrace. And blessed be the man, the lord of the land, who dealt friendly with tender Benjamin. Thus the good old man vented the gratitude of his heart, whilst his sons drew near and unladed their cattle. Very prudently had they left the carriages behind at a diftance, under proper conductors, that their father's furprife might be the lefs, until they had gently infinuated the rapturous news into his aged ear. E-very thing arrived, cattle, fervants, and ftores difpofed of properly, till a fit opportunity, the fons prefented them-felves before their venerable parent, to join him in offering up an evening oblation to that God, who had led them forth in peace, and brought them home in fafety ; for in the days of yore, the pious race delighted to ac-knowledge God for every benefit. The folemn fervice devoutly attended to, whilft gratitude and humble adorations afcended with the fmoke of the incenfe, the patriarch affembled all his family, fons, daughters and grand-children, and with an excefs of parental fondnefs embraced them all again, and enquired after what had befallen them fince their departure for Egypt. "Come Judah, faid he, you became furety for your brother Benjamin ; tell me my fon, by what means you have been enabled to fulfil your engagement ?"

"My

" My father, replied Judah, it is
with pleafure I can inform you, that
we had a fafe and pleafant journey
down to Egypt, and as foon as we arrived there we were conducted to the
prefence of the governor, whom we
found to be a fenfible and humane perfon, capable of feeling the diftreffes of
his fellow creatures. As foon as he
had by proper enquiry found that we
had fulfilled our agreement with him,
he forthwith ordered our brother Simeon to be releafed and delivered unto
us. He afked with a great deal of affection after our welfare in our abfence ; in particular for our aged father, our wives and tender offspring, in
fhort he feemed to intereft himfelf in
our concerns, as much as if he had
been our brother. You cannot think,
my father, with what delight he gazed
upon, and with what affection he embraced our brother Benjamin. He not
only returned our money for our corn,
but has been pleafed to beftow a fum,
and a fuit of apparel upon each of us,
and unto Benjamin he hath given
three

three hundred pieces of silver, and five
suits of rich apparel. Besides a very
rich and valuable present which he has
sent for you, my father, and which shall
be laid before you to morrow morning."

"Blessed be the Lord God, said
Jacob, who gave you such favour in
the sight of the man. And O may all
his kindness to you, my sons, and to
your father's house, be returned tenfold
unto him, by the mighty God of Jacob.
How causeless were my fears for you
my Benjamin ! How did my heart
tremble to think that peradventure evil
might befal you ? and I concluded,
my son, that I could not survive the
loss of you. But you know, my sons,
that my loss of Joseph might reasona-
bly make me more fearful, than otherwise I might have been. I loved him
for his mother's sake, I saw abundance
of excellencies in his opening genius,
and I thought I could see a spirit of
prophesy in the dreams he related to us.
Yet after all these things, Joseph was
torn to pieces."

" No,

" No, my father, replied Simeon, Joseph was not torn to pieces. It shall be my part now, to reveal a mystery of iniquity, which venerable Israel never could suspect his sons to have been guilty of. His dreams my father, fired the hearts of his brethren with jealousy ; and foreseing that if he lived in Canaan, we should become subject to him, we conspired against him to slay him. This was indeed our first purpose, for I have now such a sense of the evil of our proceedings, that I will not attempt to extenuate them. Reuben alone opposed the horrid deed, and thereby exposed himself to danger. Our purpose however was over-ruled, and instead of putting him to death, we sold him to Midianitish merchants. The coat dipt in blood was a contrivance of ours, to hide ourselves from a suspicion of guilt. Oh ! Sir, accuse not your sons, for it has cost us dear. Our guilt has produced the keenest remorse, and we cannot bear the frowns of an injured father." " But Joseph is not, Simeon, said the patriarch, I am bereaved of my Joseph ; and what restitution can you

U   make ?

make ? though not torn in pieces as I
fuppofed, he may be enflaved in fome
foreign country, where I fhall never embrace him." " No, Sir, replied Judah,
he is not enflaved ; we have feen him,
we have embraced him, and have con-
verfed with him. He it is that is lord
over all the Egyptian monarchy." "Oh!
what do you tell me ?" replied the patriarch, and funk down in his chair. A
little come to himfelf, faid he, " Does
Jofeph live ? Can it be poffible ? If he
lives, O that thefe withered arms could
grafp him." " Yes, my father, returned
Benjamin, he lives. Jofeph my brother,
lives ! I embraced him. He wept upon
my neck, and I on his ; and he fends you
an invitation by me, to come and fojourn with him in Egypt till the famine
is gone ; which he affures us will be five
times twelve months."

" O Benjamin, what do you fay ?
Are you affured that you now fpeak the
truth ? I faw his many coloured coat,
torn in pieces and fmeared with his
blood. How then can he yet live ?"
" Remember my father, faid Benjamin,
what Simeon has juft now declared, that
they

they killed a young goat and dipt the coat in the blood thereof, rent it, and delivered it to you, my father. So that Joseph lives, and is lord-governor of all the kingdom of Egypt. He hath befides fent waggons and other light carriages, my father, to convey you and yours down into the land of Egypt; for he tells us, that there are yet five years more of the famine to come, in which there fhall be neither earing nor reaping."

" That he lives I am thankful for, replied the patriarch; as to his grandeur it affects me not. But Joseph lives. That is enough. I will fpend the fmall remains of life in taking a journey to embrace my fon before I die. My Joseph, how have I wept over thy death my fon! But O, my God, let me but embrace him, and I fhall foon forget all the forrow fuftained upon his account. Yes, Joseph, I come to fee thee my fon. Ifrael comes to bow himfelf down upon the neck of him who was feparated from his brethren. Make ready, my fons, for our fpeedy departure. The lamp of nature is already, with me, reeling in the focket. What I
do

do muſt be quickly done, leſt death prevent me.

"But O my ſons, for your ſakes, and the ſake of my grand-children, I dread to embrace my Joſeph's invitation."— "What objections, Sir, can you have to it? There is plenty in all the land of Egypt. There is corn, wine and oil, treaſured up by Joſeph's provident care," ſaid Reuben. "It is that very plenty I dread, my ſon. And that I fear may be as injurious to your morals, as the famine might have been to your families. What, if the abundance of corn and fleſh reported to be there, ſhould incline my ſeed to ſettle in that ſtrange land, and do what they can to fruſtrate the Lord's deſign of putting you and your children in the land of Canaan. I fear for you, my children. Ye are young, and can reliſh the pleaſures of ſenſe.— Was I to go alone and viſit my ſon, the danger might be leſs; as I am old, and the pleaſure of enjoyment is departed from me." Jacob however could not reſiſt the importunity of his ſons, eſpecially Benjamin, who pleaded hard that
he

he might go and spend his days near his brother Joseph. " Well my children, I go, said he, but I adjure you by the greatest of names, that ye entertain no thoughts of settling in Egypt, nor of mixing yourselves with the children of Ham"

So early next morning he arose, he and his sons, and his sons wives and children, and departed from the neighborhood of Shalem, having first offered a morning sacrifice upon the altar El-elohe Israel, and that day reached the well of the oath, where he pitched his tent, and rested that night in the grove which Abraham planted, and where he was accustomed to offer up his devotions, morning and evening, to the Lord his God. Here also the journeying patriarch, with his family, offered sacrifices unto, and invoked the unutterable name of Jacob's God. And lo! in the second watch of the night, the tent of Israel was irradiated with celestial brightness, far surpassing the sun in his strength, and a voice not foreign to Jacob's ear, was heard to cry aloud, " Jacob, Jacob." The raptured parent of the chosen race,

U 2 replied.

replied. " Here am I. Speak Lord, for thy servant heareth.

The voice replied, " Fear not Jacob, for I am thy God, the God of thy fathers Abraham and Isaac. I have seen all thy solicitude for thy childrens' welfare, and approve thy pious regard for the promise of thy God. But know, O Jacob, that it was thy God who separated Joseph from thine embrace, to make him a nursing father to the house of Israel. I have given him glory, wealth and power in the land of Egypt for thy sake, Jacob ; that by his means, I may save the people of my covenant. Fear not, therefore, to carry thy seed down unto that land of plenty. Even there shalt thou meet thy God, O Israel, for I will go down with thee, and for thy sake will visit Egypt. There will I greatly multiply thy seed, and fulfil all that I spake unto Abraham concerning them. When I have made of thee a great nation, I will bring thy seed forth with wonders and signs in the heavens above, and in the earth below : yea, with a mighty and stretched out arm will I save thy seed, Jacob. As

for

for thee, thou shalt die in a good old age in a strange land, and thy exiled son shall bedew thy bed with tears of filial sorrow, and close thine eyes in death. Accept, therefore, of Joseph's invitation and go into Egypt, confident of the presence and protection of the God of thy fathers." Thus said, the vision departed. In the morning Jacob arose, took his sons and daughters and their little ones, their cattle and all the goods which they had procured in the land of Canaan, and journeyed towards Egypt. Greatly envigorated by the late vision, the patriarch proceeded cheerfully on his journey, till got about half way between Shechem and Memphis, when he dispatched Judah and Naphtali to court, to inform Joseph of his father's approach : and he on his part, immediately set out with a numerous train of obedient servants to meet him, and the better to expedite the journey of the Hebrew caravan. They met at the city Hieropolis, where Joseph was well known and regarded, as the saviour of Egypt. Both father and son had endeavoured upon their journey

to

to fortify their hearts for the expected interview. Yet do what they would, they could not reftrain nature from breaking through all the injunctions of reafon.—— Jofeph with lowly reverence advanced, fell down at his father's feet, and would have afked his bleffing ; but as his foul had not power to give action to his lips, Jacob would have raifed up his fon, but being overcome with rapturous joy, he funk down befide him with his head upon Jofeph's, and thus for a feafon father and fon both continued fpeechlefs, to the great fear and furprife of all the kindred company, left fuch a tide of joy, burfting in upon their hearts, fhould throw the wheels of nature off from the axis, and prove fatal to their defirable lives. At length each labouring heart vented itfelf in a flood of tears, which the father fhed upon the fon, and the fon upon the father. When the ufe of fpeech was regained, nothing was to be heard, but O my fon ! O my father ! my fon, my father, till the tide of paffion began to abate. Then both hearts were lifted up with grateful acknowledgments of

the

the goodnefs of God's holy providence, that had bleft them with a once unexpected interview. Loofed from his father's embrace, he flies to the arms of his brothers' wives, and O what endearing careffes were there betwixt him and them. O my Jofeph ! my Shuah ! my Jofeph ! my Tamar ! my Jofeph ! my Zillah, &c. &c. was all the cry. And thus they would have gone on in exchanging endearing careffes till the fun had gone down, if Judah had not put them in mind of the expediency of proceeding on their journey.

It was agreed that Jacob and his company fhould come on by eafy marches, as their ftrength and the nature of their charge would beft admit of ; and that Jofeph and fome of his brethren fhould go forward to Memphis, and inform his majefty of the patriarch's arrival. Accordingly he chofe five of his brethren and departed, and as foon as arrived, he prefented them to the king, who rejoiced exceedingly at their arrival. If Egypt, faid he, has been fuch a gainer by having only one of the Hebrew lineage, what

vaft

vaft advantages muft accrue to the land
by having all the family of Ifrael in its
poffeffion. "What is your feveral occu-
pations, my friends?" faid his majefty.
Jofeph replied for his brethren, "May it
pleafe your majefty, my brethren are all
fhepherds. From their youth up, their
whole bufinefs has been about cattle."
Jofeph chofe to anfwer for them, partly,
that by his anfwer he might pave a way
for their dwelling in Gofhen, altogether
with their father, feparated from the E-
gyptians, and partly to prevent Pharaoh
from conferring upon them honours of
ftate, or employing them in matters of
government to the diffatisfaction of the
Egyptians.

"Then Jofeph, faid the king, if your
brethren are fhepherds, I would have you
fix them in a place where they are moft
likely to find paftures for their flocks.
What think you of Gofhen, Jofeph?"
"Above all places, if it is your majefty's
pleafure, I would chufe Gofhen for their
refidence." "Very well, faid the king,
let them dwell in Gofhen. And you
fhall have letters under my fign manuel,
as your authority for fo doing."

When Jacob and his family arrived at Memphis, they were sent to Goshen, where the good old prince Potipherah waited their arrival, and had provided suitable accommodations for them, in the city of Heliopolis. Jacob went into Joseph's palace, was most affectionately received by the princess Asenath, who humbly begged the patriarchal blessing on her knees. Manasseh and Ephraim likewise came and caressed their venerable grandfather, who pressed them to his glowing bosom.

Refection received after so long a journey, and balmy rest had a little re-animated his feeble frame, Joseph took his venerable father and presented him to the king, who was struck with solemn awe at the majesty of the patriarch's person. He continued speechless for a time, till Jacob himself broke silence in the following speech. " Blessed be the Lord, the God of heaven and earth, that has raised up Pharaoh to be at this day a nursing father to many nations.— And blessed be Pharaoh of the Lord my God, who has shewed regard to my

banished

baniſhed Joſeph, and unto the ſeed of
Iſrael for Joſeph's ſake.   May thy reign
be long and proſperous, and heaven in-
ſpired peace be the poſſeſſor of thy royal breaſt.   And may that God by whom
thou now reigneſt, beſtow upon thee a
crown of righteouſneſs· in the eternal
ſkies, when thou art called to leave this
uncertain diadem to thy next ſucceſſor."
"For Joſeph's ſake, replied the king, I
embrace his father, and bid him welcome to the court of Memphis.   But
I pray thee, reverend old man, may I
be ſo free·as to aſk thine age ? I remember not that my eyes were ever ſtruck
with ſuch a venerable form."

The patriach replied, " But few and
evil have been the days of the years of
my pilgrimage ; I am now in the hundred and thirtieth year of my age ; but
the many ſorrows interwoven in my lot,
the croſs providences under which I
have grieved, have drawn old age upon
me before the time."

The aſtoniſhed monarch replied,
" What ! do you not account an hundred and thirty years an old age ? We
                                  ſhould

should think it a very extraordinary thing to see a person live so long in Egypt."

"O king, answered Jacob, to some it may appear an old age, but unto me, whose ancestors, father and grandfather, lived beyond an hundred and seventy years, it appears otherwise. Abraham, my grandfather, lived to the age of an hundred and seventy five ; and Isaac, my own father, to an hundred and eighty-five ; so that I have not attained to the lives of my fathers.

"Abraham ! said the king with some surprize ; we have a tradition concerning one Abraham, a private man, who overthrew the united strength of several kings. Are you a descendant of his ? If so, I should be glad to have an account of the truth of this affair. As I have alway considered it as almost past belief, I have given little credit to it."

"It is no fiction, my lord, returned the patriarch, the case was this. In the days of Amraphel, king of Assyria, he with other princes in alliance with him, made war with Bera, king of Sodom and the princes in alliance with
W   him ;

him ; four kings joined their forces.
together and met the five Kings of Sodom, Gomorrah, &c. in the vale of Sid-
im, where they routed the army of the
Sodomites, and made such a slaughter
amongst them, that they, finding themselves unable to make head against the
enemy, were obliged to sue for peace ;
which could not be obtained but upon
condition of becoming tributary to the
conquerors.   This they were obliged to
submit to, however reluctant.—Twelve
years they paid the stipulated sum, and
in the thirteenth year, supposing themselves in a condition to resist, they re-
fused to pay it any longer. Wherefore
the confederated Assyrians, came again
under arms and ravaged all the countries
in friendship with Sodom and Gomorrah, &c.   The Rephaims, Zuzims, E-
mims, Horites, Amalekites & Amorites,
felt the severity of their rage.   At last
the kings of Sodom having levied a numerous army went forth against them,
and joined battle in the valley of Brim-
stone-pits.   But as before the effeminate
inhabitants of Sodom, &c. could not
stand before the warlike Assyrians.—
Many

Many of them fell in the action, and the reft were totally routed. Sodom plundered and facked, and Lot, Abraham's nephew, was carried away captive. As foon as my grandfather heard of his kinfman's captivity, refolving upon his redemption, he armed three hundred and eighteen valiant young men, born in his own houfe, and purfued them unto Dan, where he found them in a carelefs and fecure manner, rioting upon the fpoils of their late conqueft. Sable night, enveloping the land in darknefs, greatly favoured his defign ; he divided his little army into three companies, two of which were ordered to fetch a compafs round and attack the camp at different places, whilft Abraham attacked it on the fide next unto him. No fooner had confternation fpread itfelf among the Affyrians, than Lot heard and knew the voice of the Hebrews.— They fet all the prifoners at liberty, and clothed them with the armour of the flaughtered Affyrians. When joining with Abraham's Hebrews, they dealt deftruction throughout the whole camp, and thoufands of the enemy bit the

ground

ground in death. Those that escaped
out of the camp sought for safety in
flight, and were pursued as far as Da-
mascus ; so effectually did Abraham follow his blow, that he rescued from the
spoilers every prisoner, and all the goods
of which they had plundered the sacked
cities, and utterly destroyed the four de-
predating tyrants." "It was always my
opinion, said the monarch, that Joseph
was descended of illustrious ancestors,
and your account of Abraham sufficient-
ly confirms it. Your family, my good
old friend, has provided a saviour for
Egypt in the person of Joseph, and it is
the least thing we can do in return, to
take care of his father's house during
the scarcity. Go, good old man, and
dwell in the land, the best of it is before
you. And you, Joseph know it is the
will of your king, that you amply provide for all your father's family and ap-
point their dwelling most agreeable to
their own inclinations."

The severity of the famine was now
felt in every part of the land, and no
provision was to be met with but what
was drawn from Joseph's granaries ;

whereby

whereby the king's exchequer became immenſely rich. For firſt he gathered up all the money in Egypt in exchange for his corn ; when money failed, he received their cattle inſtead thereof ; and when their cattle were all become the king's property, they brought their ſlaves and bondmen, and exchanged them for corn. Then they ſold every man his landed eſtate to procure bread for their mouths, and at laſt they gave up themſelves for bondmen and bond-women unto Pharaoh, in conſideration of being fed with neceſſary food. Thus the whole land of Egypt, and all that. it contained became Pharaoh's property, and no ſubject had any thing left which he could call his own.

The ſeventh year of the famine elapſ-ed, Joſeph iſſued a proclamation, invit-ing every perſon to take poſſeſſion of his alienated eſtate, to come and receive ſeed corn at the king's granaries, where-withal to ſow their fields. Now he re-turned to every man his horſes, camels, and black cattle, and all that the famine occaſioned them to part with, except their money. Only requiring that the

W 2 fifth

fifth part of the increase of all their lands should be faithfully delivered up at the royal magazines. But surely never were people more astonished than at this unexpected restitution of their estates, and restoration of their liberty, after they and all that they had were become the sole property of the king. And never was a monarch better pleased with the conduct of a minister, than Pharaoh was to see his people, by Joseph's wisdom and moderation freed from slavery, in a manner which secured the lasting dignity and affluence of the crown. To the mutual satisfaction of both prince and people, it was established by an act of state into a law, that the people should enjoy their possessions unmolested, and that the fifth part of all the increase should be Pharaoh's for ever.

It was now that Sabrina, the wife of Potiphar, was taken sick unto death ; and as she found herself confirmed in her virtue, she ventured to request a visit of Joseph, that she might have an opportunity to confess her folly to him in the presence of her husband, and implore forgiveness for the injuries he had sustained upon her account.

" O

" O Joseph ! said she, it is less shame
to confess a crime than be guilty of it.
I need not repeat the baseness of my
former guilt to you, who have been so
feelingly sensible. I wanted you now
that I might unbosom myself to you,
in the presence of my worthy lord, before I die. I admire that virtue which
made you resist the temptation I laid
for you. It has for some years been the
object of my imitation, and I think I
have felt something of its sweetness. I
can tell you : that had you complied
with my wild and unlawful desires, you
would now have been the object of my
aversion, Joseph, even as you yourself
foretold. But Oh! the virtue and honour were all yours, and the guilt, shame
and confusion my own. And can my
lord-chancellor indeed forgive the baseness of a woman who then criminally
loved him to distraction ? May Sabrina
hope that she dies under the friendship
of injured Joseph! That all resentment
is departed from his generous bosom,
and that he can freely forgive his most
violent persecutor."

" Madam, replied Joseph, my mind
is

is a ftranger to refentment : and was fo
from the firft, even when I felt moft the
power of your revenge, you was the object of my warmeft pity.   I felt it as an
evil of affliction, which it was better to
fubmit to,than to an evil of fin. I judged that the omniprefent God would by
fome means bring good out of it to me,
and therefore I chearfully, endured it.
It would, madam, be impious in an high
degree, did I forget the means by which
my God has advanced me to power, and
it would be little lefs than devilifh, to
retain revenge againft, the inftruments
he might fee meet to make ufe of. By
your means, madam, I was caft into prifon, where I met with the butler and
baker ; where alfo I firft faw my lovely
Afenath.   By their means, I was made
known unto Pharaoh, by whofe goodnefs I was raifed to power ; fo that from
the great good arifing to me from the little inconvenience I fuffered through my
then mifled miftrefs, I fhould be worfe
than an infidel, if I did not from my
heart, forgive the lady Sabrina. I rejoiced to hear of your virtue returning
to its courfe, and your affections fettled.
upon

upon their proper object, and I now rejoice to fee you in this penitent frame
of fpirit ; for whofoever confefs and for-
fake their fins, fhall find mercy."

When Jófeph returned home, he
found a poor man at his gate, foliciting
relief of his fervants. By his appearance
it feemed that he had heretofore been
bleffed with better days, for even the
ruin was noble. The fervants had each
of them contributed liberally, and a-
mongft them had made him up a purfe
of fifty pieces, and befides recommend-
ed him to the confideration of their lord.
—Jofeph's humanity was fuch, that he
never fhut his door upon the poor and
needy ; yet feldom did he relieve, before
he had properly enquired with tendernefs into the cafe. Always obferving
this rule, to put the fuppliant to as little pain as poffible.

The ftranger being introduced into
the governor's prefence, he was defired
to give fome account of the caufe of his
misfortunes.

"I am by birth, faid he, an Ifhmaelite, who traded from the land of Gilead
to Egypt. It is fome few years fince,
that

that having greatly increafed my fubftance, and added to the number of my
fervants, I ventured to feparate myfelf
from the Caravan, with which I ufually
had travelled ; fuppofing I could make
greater expedition when alone, than
when tied to the rules of the company.
But I foon found that he who maketh
hafte to be rich, fhall prefently come
to poverty ; for the very firft journey I
made with my own houfhold train, I
was befet on a fatal night by a band of
thievifh Arabs, againft whom I was not
able to make head. All my merchandize was feized, myfelf and fervants
taken prifoners, and bafely treated whilft
I continued with them. On the third
night I found an opportunity of making
my efcape, which I effected, although
not without danger. In the night I
travelled, being well acquainted with
the wildernefs, and through the day I
lurked in fome lonefome thicket, till I
got within the borders of Egypt. When
I made the beft of my way towards the
metropolis, expecting to find relief in
thofe who ftood indebted to me for
merchandize before then received.——

But

But alas ! I found there was such an univerfal infolvency among my chapmen, that I could obtain no relief at their hands. The late famine, my lord, difables many an honeft man from paying his juft debts. I have been feeking throughout the capital, and all the neighbouring towns, for an amiable young man, an Hebrew, whom I bro't down into Egypt, and fold to his lordfhip the general, near twenty years ago. As I am perfuaded, that if he lives, he fills fome high department; could I meet with him, I doubt not but I fhould find a friend in the time of my neceffity."

"What is your name, my friend? faid the governor, and what was the name of the young Hebrew?" "My name, replied he, is Alvah, and my friend's name was Jofeph, the fon of Jacob." "I am Jofeph, returned the governor. You have found your Jofeph, your young Hebrew, and I will befriend you Alvah. He faid, and flew to his friend's embrace, faying, O my Alvah! my friend, I grieve for your diftreffes, yet I rejoice that it is in the power of my hand to help you, But let me firft

pay

pay my juft debts, by returning the money you forced upon me at our parting,
Alvah." Here he ordered feven hundred pieces to be counted down, and
faid, I infift upon it if you love me my
friend, that you will accept of this as
principal and intereft, without making
any words at all about it. And do give
me a juft ftate of all the debts owing to
you by the Egyptians, and I will be
your paymafter, Alvah." Overwhelmed
with gratitude, the good old Ifhmaelite
could not fpeak a word. He hardly
knew whether the whole was not a
dream. At laft, he gave vent to the
fwellings of his heart, by fhedding a
flood of tears. Then faid, " Bleffed be
God, I have found you my fon, and you
are Jofeph ftill. Riches and grandeur
have not divorced virtue from your noble mind."

F I N I S.